LETTERS FROM THE DEAD
An Ava O'Neill Mystery

KRISTI TORKILDSON

Print ISBN 978-1-54395-277-3
eBook ISBN 978-1-54395-278-0

Cover Art By KissMyDesign

This book is dedicated to Geoff,
for always believing in me

LETTERS FROM THE DEAD

1

James Abbott, May 8th, 2015

BY MY LATEST COUNT, EIGHT COP CARS WITH FLASHING LIGHTS ARE PARKED ALL OVER MY FRONT LAWN, DESTROYING OUR OVERLY GREEN GRASS AND OUR PATHETIC FLOWER BED. Lacey never cared for gardening. She was, however, excellent at running the sprinklers in the middle of the night when nobody was watching.

There's one ambulance, even though there's no hope of survival. Two firetrucks, but no cat in a tree. Must be a slow night for crime in Highland Park. Who am I kidding? Every night is a slow night for crime in this part of Dallas.

2

Lacey Abbott, September 2014, first session

"I LOVE FRIDAYS. They are my one day "off" each week. Although...
okay, they aren't really "off". Fridays are the only day I work; okay, volunteer. I just have to get out of the house, talk to adults, do something
other than take care of my kids. Which is funny because I just love to
take care of people. I work in a hospital, did I mention that?

"Okay, you asked me about my routine. Monday through
Thursday I try to keep busy with the kids. We have play dates, go to
the park or the pool — if it's warm out — we do crafts, read books,
everything. On Fridays, I start the day with a Grande Skinny Vanilla
Latte at the Snider Plaza Starbucks (when is Presby going to put in
a Starbucks?), then I'm off to the hospital for at least eight hours of
volunteering. Each week is different, so I never really know what I'll
be doing until I get there. Friday was a bit crazy actually, because we
received our first Ebola victim. Except nobody thought he had Ebola,
or nobody wanted to think so anyway. Since I'm not a doctor or a
nurse, nobody really listens to me when I make suggestions — I mean
why would they? I didn't go to medical school. *Replenish the magazines,
wipe down armrests, help the patients turn on the tv.* This is what they use
me for, which is fine, someone needs to do it.

"But this patient, I could just feel it. He had all the symptoms, simple flu-like symptoms but they came on really fast, plus he had just been in Africa — he told me so. I voiced my concern to several doctors, but was brushed off and he was discharged anyway. And then yesterday Brandon texted me that the patient came back! This time they recognized it for what is really is, Ebola. I requested this Friday off, which I'm really annoyed about because I look forward to my day at Presby. But I can't give Ebola to my family.

"Okay, sorry, got side-tracked. I didn't set this session to tell you about the disease; I'm sure you watch the news on your own. After I leave the hospital, I head home to my kids. James usually works late, so I have dinner with the kids and occasionally our nanny, we get them all washed up and put them to bed, and then I enjoy a glass of wine, some NCIS reruns (can you believe Ziva left the show? I refuse to watch the new ones) and I wait for James. This is where it gets weird. Courtney, our nanny, started waiting for James, too. It happened right after we had the twins, who are nine months old now. All of a sudden she just wouldn't go home."

3

James, May 8th, 2015

"JACOB AND LUKE ARE MY EVERYTHING. I love Annie, don't get me wrong, my darling daughter is beautiful, but my boys, they are my legacy. There's just something about a father and his sons. Pride? Maybe. I don't know. Jacob and Luke were born on Christmas Day, 2013. I was blessed with not one Jesus, but two! Although we couldn't name them Jesus so instead we picked Jacob and Luke. Good biblical names, my parents would have been happy," I tell the annoying detective interrogating me in my own home. Detective Susie Grimm, *call me Grimm* she had said. I'm rambling, I know it, but when I get nervous I can't shut up.

"Mr. Abbott, I asked you about your wife. Tell me about your relationship with Mrs. Abbott," she replies. She's calm, almost un-fazed. This isn't her first dead body.

"I am, I am. To tell you of Lacey is to tell you of our family. We are incredibly happy, great, really," *well, functional.* "We've been married ten years," *almost faithful the entire time* "and are stronger than ever," *we are working on it.*

"And tonight?"

I take a deep breath, thinking through my every step, "Tonight was like every night. I came home around 10:00 pm and parked in the garage to avoid the rain. I put my backpack in the mudroom, poured two fingers of scotch in the kitchen, and walked into the living room. I heard the tv, figured Lacey was in there waiting for me, like she always is."

"But she wasn't."

"No, obviously she wasn't."

"But a Miss Courtney Adams was asleep on the couch?" she asks me as she checks her notes, even though she knows damn well that Courtney was asleep on the couch. I stare at the detective for a while, analyzing her as she observes me. She's tall, about five feet, seven inches I'd guess, with pale skin and shoulder-length red hair tucked behind her ears. She's wearing low-heeled pumps, tight jeans that hug athletic legs, and a bright green blouse. Her eyes hop quickly back and forth from my left to right eyes and she frowns slightly.

"Yes, Courtney is our nanny. She helps Lacey on Fridays when Lacey works at the hospital, and other days, too, when she needs an extra pair of hands. We started relying on her more after we had the twins."

"And after you discovered Miss Adams, what did you do?"

"Er, I woke her up, asked her where Lacey was, and she told me she had gone upstairs to take a bath."

"Which is where you found her?"

"Yes… The water was all discolored," I explain, remembering. "That's how I knew she wasn't sleeping. She does that a lot, takes naps in the bath. But the water. It was all wrong. And her towel wasn't neatly folded on the floor, there wasn't a towel anywhere. She never forgets to grab a towel, because she hates tip-toeing all wet across the cold floor to get to the linen closet."

The detective almost smiles at this, as if she too hates tracking wet footprints across the bathroom floor. "What did you do next? Was there anything else out of place?"

"Well," I say, thinking back. "I threw up," I mumble. I look down at my untucked shirt and slacks. Fortunately they are clean, but my cowboy boots weren't so lucky. I stare at the dried bits of vomit on the toe of my boot and shake my head. "Then I immediately called you guys. I backed out of the bathroom into our bedroom and flipped on the lights," I stand up and start pacing, "bed was made, dresser drawers were shut. Laundry was folded on the chair in the corner," I point to the corner, although we aren't in my bedroom. "I checked on Annie first, her bedroom is closest to ours. She was sound asleep. Next I checked on the twins, also sound asleep. I thanked God, because I don't think I could have rocked them to calm them down. Then I heard the sirens, and came downstairs to Courtney."

4

Lacey, October 2014, second session

"I HAD COURTNEY COME ALL DAY ON FRIDAY, EVEN THOUGH I WASN'T WORKING AT THE HOSPITAL. Instead, I spent the day sitting in my car outside James's office. He didn't leave for lunch, in fact, I never saw him at all. I felt like I was on a stakeout, though I wasn't sure what I was waiting for. What was I expecting? Courtney to show up with my kids and enjoy the day with James?

"I guess I signed up for these sessions because I needed someone to talk to. Someone else, unbiased, to tell me if our marriage is normal? James and I have a wonderful marriage. Or at least, we each have wonderful lives. Separate, but wonderful. He works a lot, enjoys making money, allows me to pursue my dreams. I love not being chained to a desk. I love being a mom. I love volunteering, taking care of everyone. James doesn't let me take care of him, though. He eats dinner before he gets home, dry cleans all his clothes; honestly, he hardly leaves a trace in the house. Other than his closet and liquor cabinet, you wouldn't know he was ever there. It's like we live completely different lives out of the same house.

"We never fight, have I mentioned that? I don't whine when he comes home late, because he doesn't complain that he has to work late. And there are cute things, too. He leaves me love notes, kisses my nose every morning and exclaims: first nose! With the same level of excitement every day. It's a silly little thing we have always done. Like the one who wakes up first takes the nose. It doesn't make sense, but it's our thing.

"You get so busy once kids are in the picture, that if you don't make the effort to make time for each other, that time just gets lost. I realize now why some of my friends say, *marriage is like sleeping next to a stranger*. They are unhappily married, obviously. I never really noticed the space between us until Courtney started staying late. It's a minor, odd behavior of hers, but the fact that I don't know how to talk to James about it, and that he doesn't seem to think it's strange, bugs me. Why can't I just tell her to leave once the kids go to bed? Why doesn't he ask what she's still doing in our house at 10 pm? And I caught him wink at her once. Are they doing this to mess with me? Is it some weird game that I don't understand?"

5

Courtney

THE FIRST TIME IT HAPPENED WAS NEW YEAR'S EVE, 2013. Jacob and Luke were finally asleep, Lacey was exhausted, we were all exhausted. Newborns are a lot of work!

I think Lacey had fallen asleep on the floor of the twin's room, but I can't really remember. All I know is she was gone, and he and I were up talking, sipping on scotch and toasting to the sweet silence of sleeping children. Before I knew what was happening, he scooped me up and laid me on the bed in the fourth bedroom. I can't even remember taking off our clothes, but I can remember how it felt that first time. It escalated so quickly, like the future of the world depended on us being together. You know what I mean? To be truly wrapped up in each other. We had become one, in a way the Abbotts had never been.

6

James, May 9th, 2015

THE DETECTIVE AND I ARE SITTING IN MY HOME OFFICE, WHICH IS RIGHT OFF THE FRONT ENTRY TO OUR HOUSE AND DIRECTLY BELOW OUR MASTER SUITE. We are both in guest chairs, a little more relaxed than if she dragged me to the station. I feel Grimm watching me as I stare out the window, watching the rain flood the lawn — it's been raining for nine days. It's 2:30 in the morning now, but I'm not remotely tired — I feel like I could never sleep again. How could someone do this? Come into my home, murder my wife, clean up and walk back out the door? I cross my left leg over my right, resting my ankle on my knee, and tap on my brown cowboy boot nervously.

"How did Courtney react when you told her?" Detective Grimm asks me.

"She froze. Literally froze. Didn't say anything, just stared at me. Through me. I still don't think she has said a word." I wish I didn't have to say anymore either.

"Everyone reacts to death differently," she says, still so calm. "Your prints are everywhere I'm sure. DNA too. It's your house, we expect that. Who else has access to your bathroom? Help us match any other prints we might find," Detective Grimm asks me.

"Um… Jacob, Luke, and Annie of course, Courtney. Lacey's brother, Rick Hopkins. Possibly others, I'm not sure. I work a lot during the week, so I don't always see who comes in and out of the house."

"Hmm," she says, clearly judging me. "Can you think of anyone who would want to hurt her?"

Cops always ask this. If I could, wouldn't I have mentioned that right away? Who would want to hurt Lacey? She's a stay-at-home mom who volunteers in a hospital. Her very nature is to help everyone. And hurt no one. Not even me, and sometimes I deserve it. "No, everyone loves Lacey," I say. Ugh I loathe myself — the widower always says that.

"We are going to need to bring Courtney in for questioning, considering she was here at the TOD."

No shit, Sherlock, I want to say, but instead I just politely nod.

"And your daughter, too."

"What? No. Detective, she's four. She couldn't have possibly done this. She can hardly lift a backpack, let alone drown an adult! You're not taking her anywhere, and anyway she left with Rick, remember?" Rick is Lacey's half-brother and only sibling. His dad married Lacey's mom when he was twelve, and they welcomed Lacey to the family one year later. While they didn't grow up very friendly towards each other, they reconnected when we had Annie and he was my first phone call after the police arrived. Needless to say, it was an extremely painful moment in our otherwise peaceful relationship.

Rick hardly spoke at all when he walked into the house, and against my advice, he wanted to see her body. His face stayed very stern, almost expressionless when they pulled back the sheet, and after a few seconds he waved his hand at the M.E., turned on his heel and

walked with me back down to my office. He had a short conversation with Detective Grimm and I helped him pack up some things for
the kids.

"Yes, I remember. James, nobody is accusing Annie of murder," the detective says after a moment of silence, "but she might
have seen something, heard something. You'd be surprised what kids
notice when you think they aren't looking." Did I imagine it, or was
there an all-knowing look associated with that sentence? A *we know all
your secrets, James* look. No, no. I definitely imagined it. She doesn't
know anything.

7

Lacey, October 2014, third session

"I CONFIDED IN BRANDON ABOUT COURTNEY STAYING UNTIL JAMES GETS HOME. Brandon just laughed, and stood up for her — *she probably just feels bad that you're always alone. So she keeps you company until your husband gets home*, that's what he said."

"Do you think that's why she stays?" asks Dr. Chung.

"No. I mean…she used to stay at my request. The twins were terrible sleepers in the beginning. I needed help. I was a zombie. I couldn't ask James to get up with them in the night, he has to go to work in the morning, you know?"

"I do," Dr. Chung Replies.

"But once the twins started sleeping though the night, I told her she could leave after bedtime. She just doesn't. She isn't keeping me company, other than being a body in the house. We don't really talk to each other after the kids are in bed. I watch tv and she texts feverishly on her cell phone the entire time. I want to scream at her to actually go and hang out with the people she's always communicating with on her phone. But millennials, that's just what they do, isn't it?"

"Millennials?"

"Sure, young adults. James is always talking about how millennials are reshaping the future with their tech-savvy-ness. She's twenty-one, prime tech-savvy age. They must think texting is the same as talking."

"Twenty-one. Interesting." She pauses, but I say nothing. Courtney's age is irrelevant. "Tell me about Brandon, you confide in him a lot."

It wasn't a question. "He's a doctor at Presby. I volunteer in his ward — Cancer Center," I added when she pierced me with that inquisitive therapist look. There's a long pause here, classic doctor-patient standoff; though I don't really have anything to hold back, so I'm not sure why I'm playing the game. "We met several years ago when I started volunteering. He's married, no kids. Works hard, but not overly so. He definitely makes time for a life."

"Is that in comparison to James?"

Wow. I guess it is, although I didn't realize it. Dr. Chung: one, Lacey: zero. "I guess so," I sheepishly reply. "But James has all the time in the world for us on weekends. Working late Monday through Friday is just his thing. But it's a schedule, a routine, so I know what to expect. Brandon's on-call a lot, so that is probably worse for his wife," I say, a little too defensively.

"Do you know his wife?"

"No, I've never seen her at the hospital. I don't see Brandon outside my volunteer hours." Even more defensive.

"James doesn't know him?"

"Of him, sure, but no, they haven't met."

"Would you like them to?"

Hmmm. *No? But not because I'm hiding them from each other. Maybe because I don't want to blend my two worlds?* I think to myself. "Sure, if they wanted. I could invite them over for dinner." I say this for the brownie points, not because it'll ever happen. *Brandon and James have nothing in common. And I probably don't with Mrs. Bennett either. Wow, what is her name? How have I never asked him her first name?*

8

Courtney

I DON'T KNOW HOW LONG IT TOOK ME TO FALL IN LOVE. Maybe five minutes. Like a storybook: love at first sight. Or, at first sexual encounter. I didn't realize life could be filled with so much passion until we got together. Maybe it was the sneaking around? Something about the thrill of being caught, but never actually trying to get caught. We were always very covert, black ops we called it. I knew his schedule like the back of my hand, and obviously I knew Lacey's, too. And setting the kids' nap times proved to be extremely helpful. We could go at it right there in the house, knowing we could never get caught. And we didn't. She died without having a clue.

9

James, May 9th, 2015

I CALLED LACEY'S BROTHER THE FOLLOWING MORNING TO MEET ME FOR A CUP OF COFFEE. Rick is an attorney, and with every passing hour I feel like I might need one. Courtney was eager to go say bye to the kids and agreed to watch them for an hour so Rick and I could visit.

Cameras at my office show my car leaving the garage at 9:45 pm, and TOD was determined to be between 8:30 pm and 9:00 pm. But, how can I prove I didn't walk out a different door on foot, kill Lacey, return to my office, then get in my car and drive home? Apparently the fact that I'm not a psychopath isn't enough. So I called Rick.

"How are you doing?" Rick asks me as he sits down and peruses the menu. He lays his umbrella on the floor and dries his pants off with a napkin. His eyes are very swollen; I can't tell if it's because of crying or lack of sleep. I think it's probably the latter, because Rick is nearly void of emotions. Twenty years as a defense attorney has basically sucked out his soul.

"How do you think? It's only been twelve hours. How are *you* doing?" I ask, but without giving him a second to respond, I continue, "Fortunately for the boys, I think they are too young to really notice. And they've really taken to Courtney, so having her around will help." I notice Rick's eyebrows raise at this. He suspects this isn't the entire truth, but he doesn't say anything, so I go on, "They won't even remember Lacey. That kills me. How was Annie last night?"

"She doesn't really understand," he says.

I choke down some coffee and stare out the window as he continues, "I think she knows what death means, but she doesn't fully realize that her mother won't be coming home."

"They did everything together," I say, then pause, wondering for the first time what they did all day. "Annie has a big dance recital next week. She will be upset her mother won't be there. It's her first recital."

"You're going to need to be at that recital, James. I'll be there too. We are going to get through this together."

I nod in response. Obviously I know I need to be at the recital. I am a single parent now. I have to step up and do the things Lacey did, too; make breakfast, go to recitals. Learn how to blend formula. Do the boys still drink formula? Mental note: buy a baby book.

"I think I'll need your help. They can't prove anything, because I didn't do anything, but I'm probably a suspect. Being an absent husband and father isn't doing me any favors." I slam the table, spilling my coffee. "Nobody ever cared that I was absent, why all of a sudden is that all people see?"

"James, please, you need to control your anger in public. If you have any emotion, it needs to be sadness or grief," Rick says, as he mops up my coffee with his already wet napkin. Sometimes he is too robotic for me. How can he not even show emotions at the death of his sister? He's a very successful attorney, I'll give him that, but really lacks social skills. He's never been married, has no children, and as far as I know, has very few friends.

"People are focused on you being absent because that's what they want to see. It's a much better story for a rich workaholic to kill his beautiful wife for no reason — cue mystery," he finger guns at me, "than to read that a jealous nanny killed her to get her out of the way. They've heard that one too many times," he finishes, rolling his eyes.

Well, that was faster than I thought. It took us ninety seconds for him to blurt out that he thinks Courtney killed Lacey because of an affair. "Jealous? Of what? A husband that's never home?" I retort.

"Of the mansion, the beautiful kids, the perfect life. You attend fancy parties, you have the latest gadgets and cars. That bitch practically drools when you walk into a room."

"Courtney is a lot of things, but she's no murderer."

"You yourself admit you're never home, how could you possibly know her well enough to judge her character?"

Trap set. I hold his glare, refusing to fall into it, "Because I just know. Lacey would have felt it, said something. She trusted her. So I trust her."

10

Lacey, fourth session, October 2014

"THE EBOLA VICTIM DIED, AND TWO NURSES CONTRACTED THE DISEASE," I START MY SESSION DISCUSSING MY WORK. I'm not sure why, but to start with facts makes it easier for me to get into the questions. "We are hoping to heal the nurses, but let's be honest, we are totally in over our heads on this one." Dr. Chung says nothing, not that I expect her to. I'm not here to talk about Ebola.

"I thought you said you work in the Cancer Center?" Dr. Chung calmly asks me.

"I do, mostly, though sometimes I'm requested in other departments. Occasionally I'm in the ER, putting new sheets on beds, preparing food, that type of thing."

"What does James think of you working in a hospital?"

"I don't think he has an opinion. Or if he does, I'm sure it's a positive one. It can be tough — losing a patient that fought so hard to survive is never easy. Sometimes I come home really broken down, but he is always there to pick me back up. And on the flip side, it can be really rewarding when someone pulls through and beats the cancer.

Being there, helping them, it really makes me feel like I'm accomplishing something useful.

"At the end of the day, I'm happy, so he's happy. We both get to do what we want, and so we support each other. Like best friends." I realize that's the problem. We are just good friends. "I don't know. Maybe we aren't in love. We love each other, sure okay, but aren't in love with each other. Is that what you think?"

"What matters is what you think."

Therapists are so annoying.

"I don't know. We've been together a long time. I can't imagine a life without him."

"Hmm. Why don't you let him join us in session?"

"Well, he had an affair." I pause, expecting a reaction that doesn't come. "He told me just over a month ago. I guess I wanted to discuss my marriage without my husband influencing the discussion." I still get nothing out of the Doc.

Have I mentioned how annoying therapists are?

"I'm wondering if it's Courtney. I thought if I told you my observations, you'd tell me if it's her." Still nothing. "He says it was a woman from work, or that he met through work. I can't remember." Silence. "The only woman I know from his work is his partner, Ava O'Neill, and it for sure wasn't her. She's definitely not interested in him that way - I know her very well. James even let me interview her before she started, wasn't that thoughtful? To make sure I approved of them working together. She and I grab coffee every now and then — no, she definitely wouldn't do this. No, not Ava. And I just don't think it's Courtney. He hardly notices her. But I don't know who else it could be. He doesn't want me to leave him, I know that much."

11

Courtney

IF I HAD TO PICK, PROBABLY THE BEST SEX IS IN THE OFFICE. Right there on the desk. The last place she would ever come to look, and yet if she looked, she would see everything. I'm sure I'm not the first, but I will be the last. Our connection is too strong. He'd never leave me, he craves me. He needs me. And she introduced us, isn't that funny? She didn't realize of course. She wasn't in love with him, she wouldn't care. I'm sure she'd be happy that he's happy! Because that's the kind of person she is.

After that first night, we tried to take it slow — had to figure out a way to stay hidden. But it got really difficult to go days without each other and we got a little sloppy, she almost caught us once. That was probably the worst day of my life. I thought I'd lose my job.

12

James, May 9th, 2015

RICK AND I HEAD DOWN TO THE STATION FOR A "MEETING," WHICH I THINK IS A NICE WORD FOR INTERROGATION. Detective Grimm greets us at the elevator and directs us into a tiny room with a rickety table, four chairs, and a one-way mirror. Yep, definitely an interrogation.

"Thank you for coming down, James, Rick, good to see you both," she opens the conversation, shaking each of our hands as she says our names. She doesn't look like she's gone home since I saw her at my place; she's in the same green blouse but her hair has been pulled up. I feel oddly embarrassed as I look down at my clean cowboy boots and fresh white shirt. "I just need to ask a few more questions, for the record, to follow up from our preliminary conversations last night and early this morning."

Neither Rick nor I say anything, both waiting our turn to be addressed a question.

"James, tell me about your relationship with Courtney Adams," she starts.

Here we go. I tell her I have almost no relationship with Courtney, other than paying her a wad of cash each month. She helps out a lot during the week, and babysits if we have an event on the weekend, but she and I hardly overlap in the house or anywhere at all. I confirm that

Lacey really likes Courtney, and so do our children. She's a role model to Annie, which we both support because Courtney is paying her way through college by doing respectable work.

"Why do you think she was still on your couch, even though the kids had been put to bed?"

"I don't know," I shrug. "Sometimes she stays late. She watches tv with Lacey. It's no big deal."

"Were they friends?"

"Lacey and Courtney? Er, no, I mean not really. But they also weren't not friends either."

"Hmmm," Grimm says. She tucks a strand of stray hair behind her ear and shifts her weight. "Seems a bit odd, doesn't it? That the kids were in bed, Lacey went up for a bath, presumably to get ready for bed herself, and Courtney just stayed on the couch."

"Maybe she had dozed off and Lacey decided not to wake her?"

"Hmmm. Maybe. Do you know if Courtney was seeing anyone?"

"I have no idea. Courtney's personal life is none of my business."

"That's an interesting perspective," Grimm says, "because it looks like you influence several of her personal decisions."

"Meaning?" I ask.

"She recently moved into an apartment only one mile from your house," Grimm says.

"So what? Plenty of people move to be closer to their work."

"Sure, but now her commute to school is nearly an hour, and presumably she's at school more than she's at your house? Not to mention, she died her hair blonde after she started working for your family, and recently started wearing blue contact lenses."

"Detective," Rick interrupts, "what are you implying?"

"I'm simply pointing out that in the last few years she has made several, ah, changes. Changes that make her look more and more like Lacey."

"Courtney looks nothing like Lacey," I growl.

"True. Being blonde with blue eyes does not make two people twins."

"Then what's your point?" I demand.

"In addition to her physical changes and her recent move — which required her to get several roommates, I might add — she has also started to take tennis lessons."

"Lots of women play tennis," Rick says.

"They do, sure, sure they do. She has also been ordering Pregnozine on Amazon."

"What's Pregnozine?" Rick and I both ask.

"It's a powder you mix into your morning water. It boosts your hormones and helps you ovulate."

"Why are you telling me this?"

"Have you ever had sex with Courtney Adams?" She bluntly asks.

I stare straight at the detective and growl, "Never."

13

Ava O'Neill, May 9th, 2015

I'M A COMMERCIAL REAL ESTATE BROKER IN DALLAS, TEXAS, AND I STARTED WORKING FOR JAMES BACK IN 2008. The market had just crashed and my previous employer sold all their office properties in Dallas, leaving me with nothing to work on, and therefore without a job. I was scrambling, unsure of what to do, when the stars aligned and James's 'twenty-something' team member moved to Houston to work for her dad's oil and gas company. The commercial real estate industry is pretty small and everyone knows everyone, so when I heard there was an opening I called James and essentially demanded he hire me. Fortunately, he did.

It was a bit of a transition for me; previously, I worked in-house for one landlord, leasing only properties we owned. I had one asset manager and he sat in the cubicle next to mine. James's team, on the other hand, does all third-party leasing and represents over ten ownership groups who live all over the country. It took a bit of time, but ultimately, I figured out each client's MO and we made a modest living during the recession.

Then, like it always does, the market started to heat back up in 2011, and the last few years have been exceptional. James and I are now principals and the top producers on QV's Agency Leasing team, and Clint Davis is the top guy in our Tenant Representation division. We have great working relationships, and at times I think they are my best friends, but only because we are at work more than we are home. James, Clint and I are all different ages and in different stages of life, so we don't hang out too much outside of the office. Actually, if I'm being honest, I don't really think James hangs out with anyone. He's a complete workaholic and is usually still pounding away when I head out each day. Today, however, he didn't show up at all.

James called me at dawn this morning to fill me in on everything that's happened to Lacey. Needless to say, I was speechless. I can't believe it, I mean, it's Lacey. She's the sweetest, most genuinely nice person I've ever met. Of all the wives, I get along with her the best. James actually had Lacey interview me to make sure she thought I would be a good fit on his team. Lacey was an excellent saleswoman; she used to sell medical devices before she stayed home with the kids. She was the best on her team, very professional and successful. He wanted her opinion, to make sure I could thrive in the third-party leasing world, and luckily for me, she gave me two thumbs up.

I usually leave the office by 5:45 every day so I can get a run in before sunset, but today I close shop at two o'clock. I'm too distracted thinking about Lacey and who could have possibly done this to her. I do my best thinking while running, so I decide to do sprints; really get the heart rate up and see where my brain goes.

After a very intense twelve-minute workout, I've come up with nothing, I've tripped in a pot hole, and my brain has gone into gridlock. I decide to call my aunt, Sally Maguire, for help.

"Fancy a glass of wine?" I say to Sally on the phone.

"At this time?" She replies.

"It's five o'clock somewhere. Shut up and let me in."

Sally is my maternal aunt. She lives two blocks away from me, in a gorgeous, two-story home that's completely paid for. She'll have a hell of a time trying to sell it though, because a few years ago she converted the entire second floor into a lab. Sally is a former forensic scientist for the FBI; she retired recently after some work-related incident that she never talks about.

"What's bothering you today?" she asks me, two glasses at the ready. I take my glass and plop down on the couch next to Rufus, her overly snuggly chocolate lab. Sally stands over us; her short blonde hair is pulled back today and at my angle she looks bald.

"James's wife, Lacey — you remember her? I think you met her at that Frisco Galleria ground-breaking event I dragged you to a few years ago? Anyway, she was murdered."

"Oh no, how? What happened?" I pick up her TV remote and flip it to the news. Unsurprisingly, a photo of the Abbotts is in the upper right-hand corner of the screen and Kailey Harris is reporting the story: *"…a complete shame. James Abbott was not available for questioning, but a source tells us that he's more than devastated. If anyone remembers seeing suspicious persons on the 7700 block of Hurst last night, please call our hotline number below…"* I mute the tv and toss the remote on the table.

"Cops think it was made to look like a suicide, though sloppily so. The killer mopped up all the water and bubbles that should have been all over the bathroom when she frailed around trying to get up for air."

"Flailed," Sally corrects me, as usual.

"What?" I ask.

"You said frailed. Frailed isn't even a word. Frail means weak, fragile. To flail is the act of thrashing around."

"Right, whatever. She flailed," I correct myself and shoot a glare at Sally. "*Anyway,* apparently our killer didn't realize you can't mop up a broken nose, which she may have received during the *flailing*." Sally pours wine into our glasses and collapses next to me on the couch.

"Jesus Christ that's terrible. How's James?" she asks.

"Not good. He found her body — threw up everywhere," I say, "he's a suspect, for obvious reasons. Been down at the station all day. They have three young children you know."

"Do you think he did it?"

"No," I reply, while taking a sip of my wine. "This is James we're talking about. James! We've worked together for years. I mean, the man doesn't have an evil bone in his body. He can't have done this, no way…" I say, then pause for a sip of wine. "They have a very young nanny," I add, "she's pretty. Too pretty; tall, blonde, beautiful, and she was in the house at the time."

"Ava, open and shut. He was banging the nanny, things got too serious and he killed his wife at the end of a lovers' quarrel," Sally says, "*or,* the nanny killed her and is hoping to take her place as wife?"

"He wasn't banging the nanny. I asked him. Yes, yes, I know he could be lying," I say after Sally nearly chokes on her wine, "but he actually told me he'd had an affair, some woman he met through work. I tried to figure out who but he's a steel trap."

"Don't you know everyone he could have met through work?"

"Yes," I say.

"Then how can you not put the pieces together?"

"There are a lot more women in commercial real estate than you'd think! Plus, it could be a broker, or a client, or a tenant. The list is endless."

"Hmmm," Sally says.

"He did confess it to Lacey; he was embarrassed, felt terrible, promised it had been one time, et cetera et cetera. Lacey started going to therapy, alone, didn't want him there — though supposedly he volunteered to join," I tell Sally, who says nothing. "I have an appointment with a Dr. Nina Chung on Monday."

"Why? What are you doing? Stay out of this."

"I can't! The detective doesn't think he's innocent, she will just form a case around him and send it off for a jury to decide. He needs me."

"First, I'm pretty sure he doesn't need your help on this. You lease office space, you don't solve crimes. And second, the therapist is going to help you how?"

"I'm hoping she will offer me some guidance," I say with a wink to Sally, knowing she hates therapists. "I'm sure she will want to help find Lacey's killer."

"Unless she *is* Lacey's killer. What we need, is to get the name of his other woman. I'm assuming you came to me hoping to do some behind-the-scenes recon upstairs, see if something doesn't fit right?"

"He won't tell me who the other woman is because he says there's no way it's her. The affair was almost a year ago, and he hasn't seen her since. And yes, to answer your question, that's exactly what I was hoping."

Sally sips on some wine and stares at me, eyebrows so high they are almost hiding in her hairline.

"I realize this looks bad. A guy admits to an affair, his wife ends up dead. But I know James, have known him for years. And his tone on the phone this morning, it was pure agony. Confusion. Slight anger. If he thought his flimsy would help, I think he would offer her up," I say.

"Floozy, you mean."

"Yeah sure, whatever, that's what I said. His floozy."

After several minutes of persuasion, Sally gives in. We top off our glasses and go upstairs to peek into the other side of James's life, a side you can only find by hacking. The lab in Sally's house is equipped with everything a stalker could possibly ask for, and what we're about to do is quite illegal. Fortunately, Sally has more protective firewalls around her programs than the CIA, FBI and Dallas PD combined.

After an hour of snooping on James, I'm happy to note that nothing sketchy really pops out. A dive into his finances tells us that he orders Jimmy Johns for lunch most days and Specs in Addison near our office is his local liquor store. His cell phone is his primary phone for both business and personal use, and there are at least thirty-five calls made and received each day, lasting a variety of lengths. All of his emails appear to be work-related, and if he has a personal email account I haven't found it.

Sally informs me that Lacey is also pretty predictable: she grocery shops at Tom Thumb nearly every day, is a Starbucks addict, only records crime shows on her tv. They pay for HBO, Cinemax, Starz, Netflix, Hulu and Showtime, but her recordings are mostly regular network. Her phone seems to be used primarily for texting, and she is in a variety of stay-at-home mom groups.

"Lacey definitely keeps busy. She is involved in more mother-child activities than I even knew existed," Sally says.

"You didn't have any kids, so who's surprised by that?"

"Excuse me, I had you," says Sally.

"You were forced to have me, that doesn't count."

"Just because I inherited you when you were eight years old doesn't mean you aren't basically my child. And anyway, I don't see any toddlers running around here," she jibes at me, as I clearly don't have any children. "But, seriously, listen to this list: Moms who cook healthy, Moms of almost-kindergarteners, Moms of Highland Park, Moms with two kids, and Moms with Nannies. Moms with Nannies? Seriously?"

We laugh at this, but it really isn't that funny. Sally got married when she was twenty-two, and shortly thereafter discovered that she and her husband were unable to have their own children. When she turned twenty-five, she and Tim got stuck with me, a vivacious pre-teen. She never complained about it though; she took me in and raised me as her own.

Three hours later, a bottle of wine down, and no closer to solving the case, we're about to call it a night when my phone rings.

"Is this Ava O'Neill?" a low, male voice says on the other end of the phone. I quickly put it on speaker so Sally can hear him, too.

"Yes," I say, "and who's this?"

"You're barking up the wrong tree. It starts with the babies." Click.

14

Lacey, fifth session, October 2014

"I THINK THE BOTTOM LINE IS THAT I DON'T WANT TO LEAVE JAMES, JUST AS HE DOESN'T WANT ME TO LEAVE," I ANNOUNCE TO DR. Chung, before I've even sat down in the chair. I had to get it out before I got too nervous, changed my mind or didn't say it. Saying things aloud to another makes it official.

"That's great news, Lacey. With a goal in mind, we can formulate a plan. What needs to change in order to solidify this decision?"

"Other than the obvious, *no more cheating on me?*" I ask her.

"Yes, other than that. We must get to the root of the issue, which will ultimately end the cheating."

"Well, I guess he probably strayed because he felt lonely. But I also feel lonely because I hardly see him and I didn't leap into someone's bed to fix that problem."

"Of course you didn't. But he did, so let's think about that."

I sit back to do as instructed. If he would come home earlier to make more of an effort with me and the children, I'd probably feel differently about our relationship. Have I been cold to him? Have I made him feel like a stranger in our house? Is that why he comes and goes without leaving a trace?

"Okay, I guess we should be more give and take. Lately, neither of us gives, and so ultimately neither takes."

"I've been tiptoeing around this question for the last four sessions, but are you two currently intimate?"

"Um… not really since the twins were born — Jesus that sounds terrible saying it out loud — they are ten months old. Twins… they are more than twice as hard as one kid, and I really struggled in the beginning. I was always asleep when James got home, and up with the babies before he woke up; sometimes we would go days without really seeing each other or talking. I guess I felt like he wasn't making an effort, so why should I? I can't do everything, I'm not superwoman."

"He can't do everything either. Don't forget that he is working all day, too."

"I haven't forgotten. Gosh no, I haven't forgotten. I'm appreciative of how hard he works, really I am. But I think I would rather have fewer *things* if it meant we had more time together. When we first met, we didn't have anything. We lived in a tiny studio apartment and we loved it! There was no scenario in which we could go days without talking. Life was easier."

15

Ava O'Neill, May 10th, 2015

I MET JAMES FOR A CUP OF COFFEE TWO DAYS AFTER THE MURDER. Two days and he hasn't been arrested, which keeps me calm, but also worried at the same time. I decide to tell him I'm going to help. We grab a table at the window and just look at each other for a while. James is only seven years older than me, but the death of his wife has already taken a toll on him. I feel like his brown hair has grayed, there are more lines on his forehead and the bags under his eyes could hold three tea bags each. He clearly hasn't been sleeping.

"You holding up all right?" I ask him, breaking the silence to start our conversation.

"Mmmmmf." He shrugs.

"I need to talk to you about Jacob and Luke," I ask him.

"Er, okay? That's sort of random... What would you like to know?"

"Are they yours?" I blurt out, and he looks at me like I've sucker punched him.

"Of course they are, how can you even ask me that?"

I sip my coffee slowly, debating how much information to share. While I don't think he murdered his wife, until we find the killer I can't be completely sure. "Would it be okay with you if I ran a DNA test?

Sally could do it, or I've looked it up online and there's a place south of downtown that can do it pretty fast and cheap."

"Ava, what the hell? Why are you even asking me this?"

"I know it seems out of the blue," I respond.

"Out of the blue!" he interrupts. "Out of the blue is an under-statement. Lacey was just murdered, Ava. This has nothing to do with the boys."

"I know, maybe, but…"

"No. You don't know. Why would you? This has never happened to you."

"James, I want to help you. That's what I'm trying to do."

"By questioning me about my sons?"

"Well," I start to explain, but James interrupts me again.

"Ava, look. The cops are working on it — just stay out of it, okay? They haven't arrested me, so they must be running down other suspects."

"Sure, maybe. I'm just trying to help, you know."

"How is this helping?"

"Well, I'm following up on a lead, you could say…it's probably nothing." I take a bite of my scone. "Question: have you ever bought a pay-as-you-go phone?"

"A burner? Like on a crime show? No."

"Hmmm." I sip more coffee. "Your bank records show that something was purchased at the Mobile Market Kiosk, and I looked into it, all they sell are pay-as-you-go phones and chargers. So I'm just wondering…where's the phone?" I look up at him, and his eyes are full of fire. For a second, I think he might slap me, but then in an instant the feeling is gone.

"This is horseshit, Ava," he says through gritted teeth. "How do you even know that?"

"Okay, fair question. Don't freak out, but Sally and I have been sort of running the case from her lab."

"Ava! Stop it. Seriously, stop it. I need you as a friend, not a damn detective. Please understand me. I didn't kill Lacey. I would never, could never, ever hurt her, or anyone for that matter. How long have we worked together?" he asks me.

"Seven years," I reply.

"Exactly. Seven years. You know me. You know I wouldn't do this."

"I know, and I'm trying to build a case to prove you're innocent. The detective doesn't care about you, if the evidence points to you, that's all she will see! Please, let me help you. I can do this, Sally basically raised me and this is what she did her entire life," I say, then repeat, "I can help you. Let me help you."

"You're just going to get in trouble. So is Sally. Let it go," he says, as he gets up and throws a five dollar bill on the table. "I'll see you later." And he walks out.

16

James, May 10th 2015

SHIT. Why did Lacey buy a burner phone? And why does Ava think the boys aren't mine? Police tape is still all over my house, but I cross it anyway and start tearing everything apart. I triple check my office, even though Lacey basically never set foot in there. I open every single cabinet in the kitchen, in the hall bathroom, the buffet in the dining room, nothing. I cross over into the laundry room and the mudroom, turn over every boot, every basket, nothing. I move over into the playroom and tear everything apart, still nothing. Where is that damn phone? After three more hours of searching all the bedrooms it occurs to me, the one place you can keep secrets safe: The place where nobody can look.

17

Ava, May 10th 2015

AFTER MY ABRUPT BREAKFAST WITH JAMES, I DECIDE TO GO BACK
OVER TO SALLY'S. I let myself in, and automatically head upstairs to
the lab. Sally's lab kind of reminds me of a space ship. The back wall
is dry-erase paint and is currently covered in my chicken scratch. The
left-hand wall has several mounted forty-eight-inch computer moni-
tors, and the right-hand side has three mounted televisions. The floor
is a silvery, almost metal looking tile, and the chairs at every computer
station are wing-backed Dr. Evil-looking seats. I pick the closest one,
kick off my converse, and sit cross-legged in the chair.

Like I do at work, I start making a list:

Why would Lacey need a burner?

- *Secret Lover?*

- *For Emergencies?*

- *To give to Someone Else?*

"Don't forget the possibility that he did buy the phone," Sally chimes
in behind me, scaring me half to death.

"Jesus! don't do that! Don't you know you can't just sneak up on
people?"

"You don't know who bought it, him or her. He could be lying so why assume it was her?" She says, ignoring me. She grabs a second seat and pulls it over next to mine.

"If she bought it for herself, maybe she knew she was in danger," I say, ignoring her in return. "Or maybe someone she knew was in danger, and they needed a secret way of contacting her. Let's loop back through her phone records and see if there are any numbers we can't match."

"This is ridiculous," she says, but she still walks over to her computer. "Why are you wanting to help him so much anyway?" Sally asks me, after about twenty minutes of focused silence.

"Because, Sally, because I can. I can do something this time — find the killer, find the answer. That's the worst part, not knowing."

"Ava, that was not your fault. You were only a child."

"Right, but now I'm not. Now I know how to help, so I will," I explain, and Sally remains silent.

After two hours of running every number Lacey called in the weeks before her death, we finally found it. "The number cannot be reach as dialed," I say, though Sally heard it on the speaker phone, too. "One call, less than one minute. A few days before her murder. This is it, we found it!"

18

Courtney

MOST DAYS, IT WAS TOO EASY. He would usually text me thirty minutes in advance, and tell me what the plan was. Sometimes all we had was a few minutes, so we would meet up in his car in the back alley when I would "take out the trash". Other times, if she was distracted watching tv, we'd be in the hall bathroom. One time it was on the front lawn! It was night time and all the lights were off, but still — the front lawn! Now that I think about it, the only time we were on a bed was that very first time. She never heard me sneak him in, or sneak him back out. It's more fun that way, don't you think?

19

James, May 10th, 2015

I'VE TEMPORARILY MOVED INTO A HOTEL ON NORTHWEST HIGHWAY AND 75, JUST A FEW MILES FROM THE HOUSE. It's a cramped two-bedroom, but I can walk to the grocery store which is great for keeping my beer fridge stocked. The downside is, in Texas is you can't by liquor on Sundays, or anywhere other than a liquor store in a wet neighborhood, and I could really use a scotch. I make a mental note to get some tomorrow and in the meantime, I crack open a beer.

My new bedroom looks like a scene from a scary movie. I have notes all over the corner table, photos and clues pinned up on the wall. A pile of crinkled clothes and a spare pair of cowboy boots sits in the corner. All I need is some string tacked up connecting various notes and I'd look the part of a serial killer.

If Lacey bought a phone, that is nowhere to be found, that means she got rid of it. Lacey never hides things, her mantra was always: *If you don't want someone to find it, throw it away.* That is how she taught Annie to hide candy wrappers from me. *If you don't want Daddy to know you had M&Ms, give me the wrapper!* she would say. Diabetes runs in our family, I was only trying to help.

If I assume she didn't actually throw it away, who, other than me, would she give a phone to? Rick doesn't have it, unless he's lying to me. Annie doesn't have it. Our safety deposit box doesn't have it. Maybe one of her friends? Jesus, I wonder what they think of me right now. I decide to call Ava.

"Hello?" she says.

"Ava, hey. I've been thinking about what you said about the phone, I think maybe Lacey bought it."

"Yes, I've been thinking that, too. Hey, I'm sorry I spun this on you, I just really want to help you."

"Sprung, Ava, you sprung it on me," I say as I clear my throat. "Look, I can't find the phone anywhere, I think she gave it to someone."

"Um well, don't be mad but —"

"You traced it?" I ask her.

"Yes," she says.

"Legally or illegally?"

"Does it matter?"

"Er - I guess not," I say.

"Do you want to know what we found?"

"Oh right, sure, of course," I say.

"There was one call within the week of her death to a burner. We think they may have been coordinating a meeting place."

"When? What day?"

"May 6th, call was at 11:13 am."

"Wednesday. Maybe they met for lunch?"

A knock on the door makes me jump. "Who is it?" I call out, "Ava, one sec, there's someone at the door." I put the phone down, but don't hang up.

"It's Mandy! James?! I just drove by your house and a cop told me I could find you here! What's going on? What's happened?!"

20

Ava, May 10th 2015

I HEAR JAMES WALK OVER AND OPEN THE DOOR. He deliberately doesn't hang up, so I continue to listen.

"Mandy – er, hey. Come in, come in," James says. I hear some shuffling and the door closes.

"James, ohmygod. Ohmygod, ohmygod, ohmygod. What happened?" Mandy says.

"Lacey was murdered. We don't really know…" James's voice cracks.

"Here," she says. James blows his nose. "Are you okay?" I don't hear James respond. "Was Lacey, you know, like, being normal, lately?"

"Er, yes. Why?"

"Oh just. Wondering. Like, nothing was going on?"

"No."

"She wasn't, like acting weird?"

"No."

"Oh. Any, like, idea who might have done this?"

"No. Not really. Did she say anything to you?"

"No," Mandy responds much too forcefully. "Nothing."

"Hey did she lend you a phone?"

"What? No, I have my own phone."

"Er, right, yeah obviously."

After some additional muffled conversation and soft sobbing, he picks up the phone.

"Sorry about that, Mandy Dillingham, Lacey's best friend," he clears his throat again, "she doesn't have the burner. She swung by the house to pick up Lacey for tennis, I guess she hasn't been watching the news."

We wrap up our call and I decide to head home. Sally searched all Lacey's bank accounts, but found no suspicious activity. Her phone records only show one call with the burner. I decide I probably need to meet with Courtney, and I make a note to see if she had the kids during lunch on the sixth. As far as Lacey's day-of-death activities, there was nothing unusual: She was at the hospital as she is every Friday. I double checked her schedule the day before, but she did nothing out of the norm then either. She woke up, took the kids to the park, back home for nap time, then took the kids to a play date with the neighbor, then back home. Neighbor's alibi checks out; entire family was eating dinner at The Dallas Club. After asking around, several witnesses saw them at the Club; and, with a subtle $100 bill, the valet manager showed me their drop-off and pick-up on camera.

It starts with the babies. What can that mean? A semi-reluctant James allowed me to send cheek swabs of him, Jacob, and Luke down to Paternity Direct on Ford Street, so I call down there to follow up on the results, but they aren't ready yet. I throw a dart at my dart board. *It starts with the babies.* If Jacob and Luke aren't James's children, then the door is open to a world of suspects. If he is, then what kind of clue is that? I pull the dart back out.

With no other leads, I decide to call Lacey's friend, Mandy
Dillingham, to see if she knows anything about the baby. She tells me
she can meet me in an hour for a cup of coffee, so I continue throwing darts.

Mandy arrives at eleven o'clock sharp. She's a beautiful curly-
haired brunette, about five foot five, with an engagement ring so big
I'm momentarily distracted. With great strength, I force myself to look
away from her hand and grab a seat. I already know she plays tennis,
but I suspect she's a runner too because she's lean, runner-lean. "Thank
you for meeting with me. James told me you are Lacey's best friend."
Clean opener, I think.

"Yes, yes I am. We grew up together, went to UT together. We've
been living, like, within a mile of each other our entire lives. I can't
believe someone would do this to her." Her eyes are really watery, but
she keeps her composure.

"What can you tell me about her relationship with James? And
her kids? Any insight you have on Courtney?"

"Lacey loves James and her kids. Courtney is, like, helpful… but
there's something a little off about her. Nobody could believe Lacey
would hire such a young nanny, but Lacey is, like, so beautiful, nobody
notices Courtney when Lacey's around. Not even James." She looked
down at her feet as she says this, and I can't decide if I should push the
subject, or wait her out. "Look. I know you work with James and are
trying to help him…I don't want to hurt him, but it'll come out anyway. Lacey was seeing someone else."

"Really? How do you know?

"She, like, blew me off last minute…we were supposed to meet
up for tennis. She'd never canceled before, so I followed her. I wanted
to know what was up."

"When was this?"

"I don't know, maybe like a few days ago? It was a rainy day, I'd just bought a new tennis skirt."

"You were going to play tennis in the rain?"

"Our club has an indoor court. We had it reserved for, like, an hour."

"Where did she go when she blew you off?"

"To a coffee shop. I think it was called Grounds? I can't remember. Anyway, she met up with a gorgeous black guy. Like really tall; strong jaw," she trails off, remembering, and I can't help but detect a tiny bit of jealousy and desire in her voice. "Do you think he could have, like, done this to her?"

"It's possible," I reply.

Mandy and I chat for another twenty minutes about the man she saw Lacey meet for a cup of coffee. She has no idea who he is, but has a lot of fun coming up with crazy ideas on how Lacey got involved in an affair. I try to point out that coffee doesn't mean anything more than coffee, but Mandy seems convinced. Once I'm confident she has nothing more to offer me, I give her my card and tell her to call my cell phone if she thinks of anything else.

21

Lacey, sixth session.
April, 2015

"SORRY IT'S BEEN SO LONG SINCE MY LAST SESSION. I got really busy once Jacob and Luke started walking — they get into everything! Ava O'Neill, James's coworker that I mentioned? Anyway he must have told her that the boys are walking because she dropped by a few weeks ago with a couple pairs of baby Nike's for them. Wasn't that nice? She's always bringing the kids gifts. Poor thing, she doesn't have any children of her own.

"Speaking of the twins, they are just so cute when they toddle around, walking right at thirteen months like their sister did. Naturally I had to start them on more play dates and activities. We started swim lessons, too, and let me tell you, Jacob loves the water. Annie is great with them, which makes my heart melt.

"Annie actually joined me at the hospital last week, which was a first for us. I try to keep her away from all of that, but she really wanted to come and practice her reading for my patients. And let me tell you, they loved her! It was adorable. She really can't read yet, but she pretends extremely well. Mr. Carter was particularly smitten — he's a newer patient. Lung cancer, poor guy isn't even a smoker, but Brandon thinks we caught it early enough and he'll pull through. Annie really hopes so because she wants to come back and read to him again.

"Things at home have been a lot better. I made James schedule some time to talk to me just like you suggested, and I really opened up about how I feel. It was a powerful conversation; I cried, he cried, we tore down the walls we had built up, and now James comes home a couple nights a week for dinner! Annie thinks it's funny, but Courtney seems annoyed by it. She doesn't like us being a happy family for some reason. James teases her about it, he treats her like a daughter — it's definitely not romantic.

"Courtney has gotten really moody. Maybe I'm starting to see her like a daughter, too, I'm not sure. She's constantly disappearing when she's supposed to be helping me at home. And when she comes back she is all disheveled and harried. She claims she's okay, but I'm worried about her.

"I tried to talk to James about it, but he just brushed it off, says it's probably none of our business. That's why I scheduled this session. How do I talk to her without pushing her away?"

22

Courtney

JAMES REALLY SCREWED EVERYTHING UP WHEN HE STARTED COM-
ING HOME FOR DINNER. He would only come once or twice a week,
but it was once or twice too many. Seeing them attempt to rekindle,
it was infuriating. The family kept getting in the way, and a girl's got
needs, you know? Having to make him dinner, buy more groceries,
clean more dishes... We had to change up our routine, and Lacey
started to notice when I was gone. Sometimes we'd be so quick, no
more than five minutes, just a little mid-day fix, I think she thought
I was outside on the phone. But other times, the passion was just too
much and I'd be gone nearly half an hour. Fortunately, she'd never
come look for me in the garage, or she would have run into us.

23

Ava, May 10th 2015

"SO WHAT HAVE WE LEARNED TODAY?" Sally asks me over our nightly wine.

She and her chocolate lab, Rufus, came over around five thirty to get caught up on the latest news with the case. My condo is significantly smaller than her house, just a two-bedroom, two-bath little place, but it is perfectly homey and warm. I like to crank down the AC all year so that I can light my fireplace, a practice that Sally refuses to understand. "It's eighty-five degrees outside, why on earth is your fireplace on?!" she says this every time. I ignore her.

"James doesn't think they really have any suspects, doesn't sound like they found any fingerprints or traces of DNA at the crime scene. Is this guy that good, or that lucky?"

"Probably a combination of both," Sally says.

"I spent a few hours going through all our active deals at work," I say.

"And?"

"And nothing. Our job is a far cry from dangerous. I thought I might be able to find an email or letter from someone threatening James, but there's nothing."

"How's Courtney?"

"Oh you know, she's a complete basket case. I talked to her today. She thinks it's her fault, being there and not hearing the intruder."

"She's kind of right though, isn't she? I mean what if she wasn't asleep. She could have called the cops, stopped it from happening."

I refill my glass and swirl it around, wondering if Courtney had been awake, what would be different? Would Lacey still be alive, or would Courtney be dead, too?

"She's related to this somehow, I just haven't figured out how yet," I say.

"It'll fall into place."

"What if it doesn't?" I ask.

Rufus jumps up onto my couch and lays his head in my lap. Technically speaking, I'm not supposed to have dogs in my unit, but Rufus is very well trained so I allow Sally to bring him over. I'm mindlessly scratching his ears, wondering how Courtney fits into all this, when Sally interrupts my thoughts.

"Your phone is ringing," she says.

"Hmm? Oh!" I snap out of my trance and pick up my vibrating phone, "Hey, James, how are you?"

"Someone ransacked my hotel room!" he yells.

24

James, May 10th 2015

EVERYTHING IN MY HOTEL ROOM IS UPSIDE DOWN. The drawers are pulled out, the mattress is flipped over. All my notes and photos are gone. At first I think I've walked into the wrong room because I don't have anything here, so what can they possibly be looking for? Detective Grimm walks in just a few minutes before Ava and Sally.

"What's missing?" Grimm asks me. She rolls up the sleeves of her olive-green blouse and holsters her gun. "Who are you?" she says to Ava as she and Sally walk through the door.

"Just my notes, I think," I reply. "Everything I could think of, every conversation, every activity within the week of her death, I wrote it all down. Photos I pulled from the house are smashed or missing. I think everything else is here, just out of place," I continue, "and this is Ava O'Neill and her aunt, Sally Maguire. Ava and I work together."

"Ava and Sally, this is a closed crime scene, you'll have to wait outside," Grimm says, nodding towards the door.

"I'd like them to stay, if that's okay?" I inform her.

"Detective, I'm Sally Maguire, I was with the FBI for nearly thirty years. I still do a little consulting work for the Bureau, when they need it. We've got gloves on," Sally says, while waving her fingers, "we aren't here to hinder the investigation, but to assist."

"Uh-huh. Okay, don't touch anything, wait over there," Grimm says, pointing to the kitchen. Ava and Sally share a glance, decide to ignore her, and follow Detective Grimm around the suite. After clearing the three tiny rooms, Sally walks around taking photos of everything.

"I can't let you take photos," Grimm says.

"Well if it isn't Sally Maguire," says an older black man standing in my doorway. He has a military haircut and a toothpick in his mouth.

"Brooks! What are you doing here?" Sally responds, walking over and giving him a hug.

"*Captain* Brooks, actually," he says, puffing out his chest.

"Excuse me, *Captain*, so rude of me," she replies, bowing. They both laugh and hug a second time.

"Grimm here is my top detective, and with this being a pretty high-profile case, I thought I'd drop in."

"Fantastic! Mind if we snap some photos and take some notes? I promise we won't send anything to the press — we are here on behalf of James Abbott and his privacy is top priority."

"For you, anything. And who's this?" Brooks says, looking at Ava.

"My niece, Ava O'Neill. She works with James."

"Ah, Ms. O'Neill, I haven't seen you in years. Look at you all grown up!" He exclaims, while shaking Ava's hand. "Your aunt and I were rookies together, back before she joined the big leagues."

"Please, call me Ava. Good to see you again — and thanks for letting us stay."

"Grimm," Brooks says, "you can trust these two. Let them help, but don't let them hinder."

Grimm grumbles a little but doesn't push the subject. She tightens the tuck on her green shirt before beckoning to Sally. "Let's start in here," she says. They walk around my bedroom snapping photos and taking measurements, then she points to the mattress. Sally gives her the thumbs up and Grimm flips it over back onto the bed. That's where I see what I had missed before: bullet holes.

"Sally, is it? Come snap a photo of this. Looks like we have some brass here," she says, lightly tapping the bullet shells with her foot. "CSU crews will be here in a second to dig the bullets out of the mattress."

Sally does as she is instructed and takes several photos of the brass. It's slightly odd to watch the young detective boss around this older woman, but I'm just glad they have come to a silent acceptance of each other. I'm guessing Sally is closing in on fifty. She has dyed blonde hair that's perfectly curled in a short haircut and bright, green eyes. She's wearing leggings that show off her great shape and feed into a pair of chunky combat boots, topped off with a baggy sweater, hiding her tiny waist and large chest. I look over at Ava, who's wearing extremely worn converse sneakers, and I realize I don't usually see her dressed in anything other than work attire. It almost makes me laugh to see her at her normal height, because at work she only wears four-inch stiletto-type heels and meets me at eye level. Flat footed, she's a few inches taller than her aunt, and completely opposite in looks. Ava has long brown hair, big blue eyes and dark eyebrows.

"Whoa — someone tried to shoot you?" Ava asks.

"What's the brass say? Luger? Looks like nine-mils," Sally asks.

"Yep, reloadable. Nice stuff." Grimm holds up the brass so I can see, and I nod acknowledgement of its perfect shape, "Why would someone double tap the bed if you weren't in it?"

I could feel my jaw drop, stunned at my own realization. "Maybe they thought I was in it," I reply, staring at my feet. "I've slept in the same bed as my wife for twelve years. We weren't perfect, no, but we slept together every night, no matter what." The girls say nothing, but continue staring at me. "I bought a full-size body pillow. I've been holding it at night as comfort. I left it under the covers, so to the shooter, it may have looked like I was in the bed." And in spite of myself, a tear falls down my face.

25

Ava, May 10th, 2015

I TURN AWAY FROM JAMES, PRETENDING I DON'T NOTICE HE'S CRY-
ING. The man is in shock, he needs some time to himself. The body
pillow is on the floor, feathers popping out from where the bullets flew
through it. I bag a few feathers, mostly just to keep busy while waiting
for the CSU crew to arrive with a full crime scene kit. Protocol requires
them to use an adhesive lifter on James's hands to check for gunpowder
and confirm he didn't do all this himself. I hold my breath during the
process, praying he is clean. Thankfully, he is. I take a breath.

"So you sworted them with a pillow, eh?" I say to James, trying
to lighten the mood.

"Sworted?" Grimm asks.

"She means *thwarted*," Sally corrects her.

"Same thing," I say.

"No it isn't," Sally says.

"Someone came in here, thought they shot you," Grimm says,
ignoring Sally and me. "Then they realized it wasn't you, and tore the
place apart," Grimm continues, mostly to herself.

"They must have used a silencer," I say, playing the part of detective. "If they fired two rounds, and then had enough time to cause all
this mess, they knew nobody could hear them."

"Sig Sauer pistol and silencer then. Best 9-mil silencer on the market," Sally chimes in.

"Personally, I like my Glock Seventeen," Grimm says, while tapping her hip, "and all the noise it makes."

"Why would someone come after us?" James asks, back on target, "we don't owe anyone money. We've never hurt anyone. Never had a run-in with the law, nothing. This doesn't make any sense," James finishes, panting slightly.

"Where are your kids?" I ask him, suddenly aware they aren't here.

"Rick drove them down to Austin, to stay with Lacey's parents. Until we find her kil– until we solve the case. They aren't listed, the kids are safe there."

I want to point out that this hotel isn't listed as his address either, but decide to keep that to myself.

"Okay, that's good, keep them there. You can come stay with me — my building is much more secure than this piece of crap," I offer, to the surprise of everyone in the room, "if you want to, that is. No pressure," I add.

He nods in agreement, and Sally and I take James from the scene, leaving CSU and Detective Grimm to finish bagging and tagging the room.

26

James, May 10th, 2015

IN ALL THE YEARS I'VE WORKED WITH AVA, I'VE NEVER BEEN INSIDE HER HOME. It's pretty close to my house, just a mile or two, but we rarely schedule activities outside work. She gets me settled on her couch and puts on a pot of water. Why do people always think you want tea after a disaster? I hate tea. I really want to tell her this.

"This is for my hot water bottle," she says, as if she can read my mind, "I twisted my ankle while running the other day — pot hole snuck up on me. All this rain we've been having…my running glasses get foggy and sometimes it's hard to see."

"Er — right," I say. "Why don't you just run on a treadmill?"

"They're boring," she says with a shrug. "The heat helps with the swelling. It's already loads better than it was. Scotch, right? I have some old Glenlivet in the cabinet, will that do?"

"You're an angel," I reply. Damn, that's awkward, I wish I hadn't said that.

While she's rummaging around in the kitchen, I start to look around. Her condo is really nice; clearly this is a high-end building, though I can't figure out why she'd rather live here than in a house. Ava made almost a million last year; she can definitely afford a bigger place. The front door opens into a huge kitchen with dark brown cabinets and a large island with a glossy granite countertop. The living room has a pass-through fireplace that goes into what is probably supposed to be a small dining room, but instead is being used as a bar, complete with kegerator, wine rack, and several bottles of liquor. I can see two bedrooms, one on each side of the apartment. We are on the third floor and we came up the freight elevator from the garage, but I'd bet there's a nice lobby and doorman.

"I feel safer in a building than in a detached single-family home," she says, reading my mind again. "It's just me, no guard dog or anything. All my neighbors are sixty-plus years old. It's like Fort Knox trying to break in here, can't find a better building in Dallas."

"You spend too much time in buildings," I reply, though that seems like a stupid thing to say. Ava and I both lease office space for a living.

"Well, I like them," she says, with a tone of finality. She hands me the scotch, and sips on red wine.

"Thank you," I say as I take the glass, "you don't seem like the type that would drink this."

"I'm not. I don't. It was left here, probably from a party or something," she says with a wave of her hand.

It was an obvious lie, but I decide not to push it. We sit in silence for a while after that, a comfortable silence, but a silence still.

"An old boyfriend left it here. You probably figured that out already. Turns out, he was married. Men are terrible," she says, while shaking her head.

"Which boyfriend was this?" I ask, rather rudely. Why can't I keep my mouth shut today?

While she thinks about my question, I realize that I don't know much about Ava's personal life. She's a hell of a leasing agent and her clients love her. That seemed like all I needed to know about her. But now she is just staring at me like I'm an idiot.

"Mark. I brought him to the Christmas party this year? Should have figured it out sooner, but I try to keep Sally from looking up phone records, bank statements, criminal records, and marriage licenses every time I go on a date. It takes all the fun out of it." She pauses, staring at her wine, "If you know everything up front, the dates are really boring." Then she laughs, clearly remembering a specific incident. Her laugh gives me goosebumps, and it's a pretty warm apartment. Will I ever laugh again?

"How did you confront him?"

"It was easy actually. I was sitting right here, and his phone started ringing on the coffee table. He was in the shower, so I glanced at the screen and saw it was his wife. Guess what her name is in his phone?" she pauses for reaction, "*Wifey*. I nearly threw up just reading it. He isn't Australian, there's no need to call her a *wifey*. I would've ditched him just for using such a stupid slang, but the marriage thing was a better argument." She laughs again. "I pulled a Rachel from *Friends* and threw all his stuff over the balcony. Like she does to Paolo, you know? And he got out of the shower and had nothing to wear. So I lent him a little short dress and sent him on his way."

I crack a smile, but can't quite get a laugh, just picturing Mark scooting out in a tiny black dress past a bunch of eighty-year-old women.

27

Ava, May 11th, 2015

TODAY I HAVE MY APPOINTMENT WITH LACEY'S THERAPIST, DR. CHUNG. Her practice is in a small, quaint office building in Richardson, the city northeast of Dallas. I actually previously leased the building for an ownership group based in Chicago, but they sold it in 2012 to a firm that does all in-house work. I don't remember the therapist; she must be a recent addition to the tenant list.

It only takes fifteen minutes to get to the building, so I decide to swing through the drive-thru Starbucks in the new State Farm CityLine development, and circle back to the building. I still have twenty minutes to spare, but I head in anyway and scope out the scene in her waiting room.

Her office is on the fourth floor overlooking the Spring Creek Trail and Nature Preserve. The view up here is beautiful. It's the only window angle in the building that doesn't look over the freeway or the other surrounding properties. *She must have picked this suite for the tranquil view*, I think to myself.

"Ava O'Neill? The Doctor will see you now," says her admin, pointing towards the door on my right.

I head through the door and meet the admin on the other side. We pass an elderly man in the hall, and he smiles at me and nods his head. "Good morning!" he says.

"Morning," I reply with a smile. I am warmed by his demeanor and the brown and green tones the doctor chose in her carpeting, paint and furniture. Everything is perfectly selected to match the view out the window.

"See you next week, Allen," the admin says to the man.

"Looking forward to it, dear," he responds.

I follow the admin to the fourth door on the left. In Dr. Chung's office, there's no couch for me to lie on. I feel slightly cheated, but say nothing as I take a seat in front of her desk.

"Good Morning, Ms. O'Neill." She extends a hand to me.

"Morning, Dr. Chung, thank you for seeing me on such short notice." I take her hand.

"Please, sit, sit. I see you already have coffee, can I get you anything else? Water? A snack?"

"No, thank you I'm fine. I am actually here to discuss Lacey Abbott."

"Oh!" she exclaims. "I caught a piece of her story on the news. Are you a police officer?"

"No, no, nothing like that. I'm a concerned citizen and a friend of the family. I'm trying to help her husband, James, find her killer."

"It's a terrible sadness, what happened to sweet Lacey, but I'm not sure I'll be able to help you; doctor-patient privilege and all."

I nod, but she isn't paying attention to me anymore — she is glancing out the window now, seemingly lost in thought. "I understand," I say. "If I step out of line in my questioning, let me know. I've worked with her husband for several years and I'm just trying to help him out. I want to help him find who did this. I want to help him get closure." Dr. Chung says nothing, so I continue, "I was wondering what you could tell me about your sessions with her? Her calendar reveals she saw you eight times."

"Seven actually, she never made it to the last one," Dr. Chung responds.

I look at my notes and see that her eighth appointment was scheduled the morning of her death. "Really? Did she call to cancel it? She didn't remove it from her schedule."

"It was very strange. Very strange," she trails off, thinking. "After our seventh visit, she told me she had gained all she could from therapy. She never requested any prescriptions, and in my professional opinion, she didn't need any. She just wanted to talk to someone who didn't know anyone in her *circle*. And after her seventh visit, she said she was in a good place, centered. She thanked me for my time, even gave me a gift. Patients never give me gifts." She looks over at the salt lamp on her side table. "*Every good juju-filled room needs a salt lamp*, that's what her note said. It's a wonderful lamp."

"Yes it's very lovely, definitely adds something," I talk slowly, not trying to rush to my next question. "If she had no intention of returning, why did she schedule the eighth session?"

"Well, that's what is so strange. She called me the day before, said she had learned something terrible, and had to see me, my first slot the next day. *Do whatever you have to do to squeeze me in,* her message said. I did. She didn't come."

We both sit and think about this for a while. She learned something, was frantic, but wanted to share it with someone who knew nobody in her life. Why? Several minutes later, Dr. Chung breaks the silence.

"How is James?"

"Not great. Someone tried to kill him yesterday — shot up his hotel room."

"A shooting? I didn't see that in the news!" She is oddly excited about this.

"The cops were able to keep the media out of that one, so please keep this between us."

"Of course, of course," she says, slightly shaking her head. "It's odd, though, isn't it? Two methods of murder. One so personal, one so distant. Do you think it's the same killer?"

"Actually, I hadn't considered the idea it could be two killers," I say, kicking myself for not thinking of this. I guess that's why I'm not actually a detective. "A woman dies and two days later there's an attack on the husband, seems clinked."

"Clinked?"

"Yeah, or no, that's not what I meant. At first I was going to say connected, and then I decided to say linked. Came out clinked."

"Right. Well, yes, it probably is *clinked*. Lacey's murder might not have provided the closure the killer thought it would. Clearly, Lacey was the target. James is an after-thought. Or a loose end."

She says this with such a matter-of-fact way that something Sally said to me rings in my ear: *unless she is the killer.*

28

James, May 11th, 2015

STAYING AT AVA'S IS ODDLY CALMING, AND I WONDER HOW OFTEN SHE HAS PEOPLE TO STAY WITH HER. Her guest room is the perfect guest room, complete with a body pillow. She has a jar of sample-size toiletries and a drawer full of new toothbrushes in the bathroom. There are twenty empty hangers in the closet; I suppose those are for longer term guests. A frame on the side table displays the wi-fi password, and there's a basket full of blankets next to the queen size bed. Originally, I planned to just stay the one night, but that's about to be two, and it's so welcoming that I wonder if she'd mind if I stayed a little longer. I pull on some clean jeans, a white tee, my brown cowboy boots, and prepare for another day.

"You are welcome to stay here for a few days, if you'd like," she says, greeting me in the kitchen. "Coffee?"

"Please," I reply, starting to wonder if she really is a psychic in addition to a real estate broker. I plop down on a bar stool while the Keurig makes my coffee. "You have a wonderful guest room, very comfy bed."

She laughs at this, and again I find myself drawn to her laughter. How have I never noticed it before? "Usually, it's empty. But I saw on Pinterest how to create the perfect oasis for guests, and I really jumped on it. The only person to ever stay here is Sally, so really you are my first guest."

Her first guest. So it's not a revolving door. Mental note: get a thank-you gift for Ava.

"Er – so, how was Dr. Chung yesterday? I tried to stay up to see you last night, but exhaustion took over. I think I fell asleep at seven pm. I've never done that before."

"She's interesting. Typical therapist," she says with a shrug. "She wouldn't give me a copy of her notes, but she did tell me that her sessions were almost exclusively to discuss her volunteering and her relationships with you and Courtney."

"Did she think Lacey was doing better?"

She pauses at this, debating. "Yes and no… After her seventh session, she said Lacey was done with therapy, that she was on the right track and knew what she wanted in life going forward. But then she scheduled an eighth session under suspicious conditions, and she skipped it."

"She skipped it? Why?"

"I don't know. She just didn't show up at all, with no notice. Oh also, I thought you should know, Courtney was with Annie and the boys at the park during lunch on the sixth. She said Lacey needed to run a few quick errands and the kids would have slowed her down."

29

Ava, May 11th, 2015

I ALREADY KNEW ABOUT JAMES' AFFAIR AND HAD WORRIED ABOUT
THE COURTNEY-JAMES-LACEY TRIANGLE BEING A PROBLEM. But
when I met with Courtney, she seemed so stunned by the situation.
She was also really mad at herself for sleeping through the murder
and seemed to hold herself partly responsible for Lacey's death. She
sobbed basically the entire time, real tears. Ugly tears. Hard to fake
tears. At this point, I'd be really surprised if she and James had been
sleeping together.

I watch James closely as I tell him about my visit with Dr.
Chung. He doesn't seem surprised by the information; he seems more
confused. I don't really know what else to say to him, and Sally texted
me with a lead, so I leave him at my place and head out of the condo.

"I have two treats for you," Sally says as she opens the door. Her
blonde hair is already curled and her combat boots are on. "Which do
you want first, the fun fact or our next lead?"

"Fun fact," I say, as I step into her house.

"The blood test came back on Lacey — no drugs in her system, no diseases, not pregnant," she says. "Not pregnant," she repeats.
"Meaning, it isn't new babies."

"How do you know that?"

"I called Brooks after our little rendezvous at James's hotel room, and we met for a drink. We agreed to keep each other in the loop as we learn things, off the record of course."

"Of course," I parrot.

I walk into Sally's kitchen to make a cup of coffee, and wonder how these mysterious babies fit into the picture. *If they are not Lacey's babies, whose babies are they and how does they affect James?*

Rufus trots over and starts sniffing me, concerned I may have been cheating on him with another dog. Once he decides I haven't been, I bend over to pet him. I'm mindlessly scratching his ears, wondering who James might have gotten pregnant and waiting for my coffee to brew, when Sally interrupts my thoughts.

"Don't you want to hear our next lead?" she asks.

"Oh!" I snap out of my trance, "yes, duh, what is it?"

"Her meeting on the sixth — they met for lunch, Matza Kitchen on Walnut Hill, bill was $52.68, a little high if she was eating alone," Sally says to me. "She eats there about once a week, so it didn't pop out to me on my first dive through her bank records. I think we should go over there. See if the staff remembers who she was with."

"Absolutely," I say, "but after I finish this coffee."

"Rough night?"

"More like a rough morning." Sally nods and doesn't push the subject. We finish our coffees in silence, give Rufus a kiss and scoot over to Matza.

Matza Kitchen is about five minutes from Sally's house. We score a spot right in front and walk straight up to the front door. It's locked; the restaurant doesn't open until ten thirty. I knock, loudly, and, after about thirty seconds of pounding, someone pops out of the kitchen to see who is making all the noise.

"Hi," I shout, holding up a photo of Lacey. "Will you let us in for a few minutes?"

The man nods and comes to let us in. "We don't open for a few hours, can I help you with something?"

"I hope so! I'm Ava O'Neill… I'm um, a reporter for the *Dallas Business Journal*. I've heard that Lacey Abbott was a regular here? Do you happen to know her?" I ask, inviting myself in and taking a seat at the first table. Sally looks at me like I'm an alien, but doesn't ruin my fake story.

"Of course! Lacey is a regular, eats here every week. Quinoa Salad, no chicken. And she covers it in salt. She comes in every Friday, we have her bowl ready at eleven fifty."

"I was wondering if you saw her last Wednesday, did she eat here with anyone?"

He laughs to himself before answering, "She said she couldn't make it on Friday so she had to get her *fix* a few days early. She was dining with some black guy. Really tall, like a basketball player. Huge hands," he says, holding out his hands. "He broke his water glass — squeezed it too tight," he adds, when Sally makes a noise. "I'd seen him before, not sure his name, though. But you always remember someone that tall. Ducks to get in the door," he chuckles while ducking his head, as if he too has to duck to get in the door. "Is Lacey okay? Why are you writing an article about her?"

"She was murdered, actually," I say, and he nearly slips from his chair. "I wonder why she couldn't come in on Friday, she was working that day, doesn't make sense," I say to Sally. "She could walk here from the hospital, probably why she comes in every Friday. But why skip her last Friday? That seems pecuniary."

"Almost had it. I think you meant 'peculiar'?"

"Yeah, whatever! It's *peculiar*. Better?"

"Better. Maybe her superior at the hospital lied, and she wasn't really volunteering that day," Sally says.

This is why I love Sally. Never assume you're told the truth. "Thank you for letting us in, we will have to come back for a quinoa salad sometime."

"Sure, yeah," he says. His face is pure sadness and he looks down at the floor. "I'll be here."

"If I have any more questions, I'll give you a call," I say to the man. We exchange numbers and I walk out the door.

30

James, May 11th, 2015

I POST UP WITH MY COFFEE AND A USB DRIVE OF EVERYTHING I COULD PULL FROM LACEY'S COMPUTER BEFORE IT WAS TAKEN AWAY, READY TO FIND A CLUE. I plug it in to Ava's home computer and tap my fingers on the counter, waiting for the disc icon. Once the drive loads, I take a look at Lacey's Pictures folder, but I start crying so intensely I have to push it away. Seeing photos of Lacey smiling, playing with the kids…it's like losing her all over again. I want to kick myself for ruining her trust, for straying. One stupid mistake sent her to seven therapy sessions to decide if she wanted to stay with me. I should have always come home for dinner. I should have helped her cook, bought groceries, asked her about her day. Told her how much I loved her, appreciated her, and needed her. She was perfect.

I walk several circles around Ava's kitchen before diving back in. I take a deep breath and step back over to the computer. After half an hour of scrolling through photos and videos I've learned nothing. *What do I do now?* I ask myself. I decide to log in to her Gmail account to see if there's anything suspicious there.

Marriage is a strange relationship. You have access to everything the other person owns: their money, their house, their cars, their phones, photos and emails. And yet, I think in most marriages, you don't actually intrude on their things. I almost never drove her car or used her phone, because why would I when I had my own? I paid her credit card bill without even looking at it — I have no idea what she was buying all the time. And I can say with confidence that I never logged in to her email during our entire marriage. We both used the same password for everything, so I could have checked her email at any time; I just never felt like I needed to.

Her Gmail turns out to be a really boring read. It's mostly full of notifications from NextDoor, our neighborhood-watch app, and updates from her clubs. What I really need is her phone, but I have no way of accessing it because the cops took it. And then it hits me — her iPad. Her iPad is connected to her phone, and I borrowed it for work the other day because mine was malfunctioning.

I leave a note on the counter for Ava and speed off to my office.

31

Ava, May 11th, 2015

SALLY AND I DRIVE ACROSS THE STREET TO PRESBYTERIAN HOSPITAL'S CANCER CENTER, DISCUSSING THIS MYSTERIOUS BLACK GUY THAT LACEY MET WITH FOR COFFEE AND THEN FOR LUNCH. At the check-in counter, we ask where Volunteers sign-in. The young, hipster looking girl behind the front desk points us toward a door down the hall without even looking up from her computer. We follow her directions and head toward the door.

"We're looking for Vivian Wood," I say to the woman behind the Volunteers desk.

"That would be me! Call me Viv. Are y'all first-timers?" Vivian asks in a way-too-excited southern accent. Her hot pink blouse matches her pink scrunchie and I stifle a laugh.

"Sort of. I'm Ava O'Neill, we spoke on the phone a few days ago?" I say. "I called about Lacey Abbott?" I add, because she's looking at me like I'm an alien.

"Oh! Erm, yes, dreadful thing to happen to Mrs. Abbott. She was our best volunteer you know, worked here five years this fall."

"We wanted to confirm she was here all day on Friday the eighth. She missed her lunch appointment, so we are double checking all our notes."

Vivian flips through the sign-in book, and points to her entry on the eighth. "You can see right here, she signed in at nine fifteen am."

"Did you actually see her?"

"Erm, well, no. I couldn't make it in that day. But we had all regulars on the schedule for Friday, so I knew they could get on without me," she says, looking a little flustered.

"Is there anyone here today that could confirm whether she was here on Friday?" Sally asks.

"Ava! Hey!"

I turn around and see James walking toward me. "Hey!" I respond in surprise.

"You and I must have had the same idea," James calls out, as he walks through the door.

"Confirming Lacey was here on the eighth?" I ask him.

"Oh, well, no."

"James, is this Lacey's signature?" I ask, interrupting him. He jogs over and looks at the book.

"Er, no, no it isn't."

"Hmm. Who else has access to this book?"

"Anyone," Vivian says. "Unless someone is sitting here. We just tuck it in this nook here, it's just a volunteer sign-in book," she says a little defensively.

"Can we speak to Dr. Bennett?" James asks.

"Oh Dr. Bennett isn't here right now." Vivian giggles. "Is there another doctor I can get for you?"

"When will he be back?" James and I say in unison.

"Not for a few days, I'm afraid. He's not well."

I glance at James, and notice his face is turning red. "Where can we find him? It's an emergency," Sally says, seeing James' forehead start to sweat.

"I'm not sure, actually, he isn't home. We sent him a box of Tiff's Treats, you know, the cookie delivery? To help him feel better. But nobody answered the door…they brought the cookies here," she looks over to a half-eaten box of cookies. "The nurses have been coming by to eat them, I swear I haven't had but one cookie," Vivian says, with a somewhat guilty expression on her face.

"How do we find him?" James demands.

"I don't know," Vivian says.

"Vivian, here's my card. Call me if he comes in, will you?" I say.

"It's extremely important that you call us okay?" James says. "Do not, I repeat, do not, forget. Understand?"

"Yes, yes of course," she mumbles, taking the card from me. I grab James by the elbow and steer him outside.

"You thinking what I'm thinking?" he asks me.

"I'm thinking it's odd that someone signed Lacey in. Who's Doctor Bennett anyway?"

"Doctor Brandon Bennett killed Lacey," James declares.

32

Lacey, seventh session, April 2015

"COURTNEY HAS BEEN OUT SICK WITH THE FLU. I mean who gets the flu in the summer? She has to be the only person. Surprisingly, I miss having her around — her odd little behaviors. The kids miss her, too, they find her fascinating. Or at least, Annie does. They play dress up a lot, put on plays for me and the boys. They laugh, though they have no idea what the girls are doing.

"James doesn't seem to have noticed she isn't around. He did ask once if she was okay, and when I told him it was the flu all he said was *oh, bummer.* Then he started talking about some new office deal he was working on in Uptown and I tuned out. I think it's great how passionate he is about office space, but personally I find it quite boring. A law firm decided to put all the attorneys in cubicles, can you believe it?! CUBICLES! I tell him I can't believe it, how will they slam the door on a client? And we laugh. But really, who cares if they are in cubicles?

"I guess it mattered because this furniture decision caused their square footage to shrink in half, and with it his commission... So I guess that was a bad day at work. But hey, at least we found a way to laugh about it, right? Anyway, that's not important.

"The hospital has been pretty mellow and nobody even remembers the Ebola incident anymore. All the patients I am helping are making great recovery, which Brandon is happy about, too, for obvious reasons. He's had a real skip in his step lately, and I'm telling you, it's infectious, and honestly I'm just feeling really good about everything. The hospital has been rewarding, James is making a better effort at home. Annie is excited about starting Kindergarten this fall. Honestly, what more could I ask for?

"Talking with you has helped me remember how much I love James. It might not be the same love as when we were younger, but we hold each other up. Support each other. We have a happy family, and really, that is all that matters to me.

"Oh, I almost forgot. I lied to you once, back in the beginning. Brandon has been to my house before, he stopped by right after the twins were born. It was New Year's Eve, actually. It was a quick visit, just to check in on me…the birth was a bit traumatic – I had to have an emergency C-section. Anyway, I delivered at Presby so obviously the word spread and Brandon heard about it. He brought flowers and two teddy bears for Jacob and Luke. James wasn't home, he was closing a deal at the office, so they didn't meet. But I have seen him outside the office, and I had told you I hadn't. I don't know why I feel like it matters, but I just thought I should tell you. I couldn't leave here knowing I had lied, no matter how insignificant."

33

James, May 11th, 2015

I'M BREATHING VERY DEEPLY, AS IF I'D BEEN RUNNING, WHEN REALLY I HAVE HARDLY MOVED IN THE LAST TEN MINUTES. Ava is just staring at me, waiting for an explanation, or evidence, to prove my accusation.

"He's been in my home, Ava, do you know what it feels like to hear something like that? She confided in him when she couldn't with me. A man I'd hardly ever heard about, came to my house to check on my wife and children."

Ava continues to stare at me, so I just stare back at her. She's chewing the inside of her cheek, like she always does when she's thinking.

"How do you know that? Were you there?"

"Er, no, no I wasn't. I was with you and Clint, actually. It was just a few days after Jacob and Luke were born, and we were running a fire drill for Legend Commercial, remember that?"

"Oh, yeah sure, last Christmas. Why is that relevant now?"

"I just snuck up to the office to get her iPad. Remember how I borrowed it last Monday for the McKinley tour? Anyway, last week she texted Brandon a photo of Jacob with a teddy bear, and a note that said, *It's still his favorite!* and he responded *Best NYE Ever J say hi to the little man for me.* His best New Year's Eve ever was with my family? What kind of crap is that?"

"Not to interrupt, but you're making quite the assumption. Why don't we do a little drive-by of Dr. Bennett's house, and ask him ourselves?" Sally says. I roll my eyes a little, as she clearly isn't understanding me, but mid eye-roll, I think better of it and stare at the ground. Ava's phone rings, she holds up her index finger and answers the phone.

"Ava O'Neill," She says. "Uh huh," she pauses, listening, "that's great, thank you for pushing it through." She hangs up and turns to me.

"That was Paternity Direct. The twins are, in fact, your sons."

"No effing way!" Sally announces.

"Excuse me?" I say to her.

"You didn't tell him?" Sally says to Ava.

"Well, no, not everything…I was following up on a lead, now we have an answer. Door is shut on that line of suspects," Ava says to Sally.

Sally rolls her eyes at Ava and walks away from us to make a call. While we wait on Sally to come back, Ava tells me about the anonymous phone call she received a few days ago.

"What the hell? *It starts with the babies?* What Babies? My babies? Why didn't you tell me this before?" I ask her. I think about this for another second and it dawns on me, "Oh god, oh no, oh god, was Lacey, was Lacey —"

"No, she wasn't. We already got her blood work back," Ava reassures me.

I sigh in relief. "What can that mean then?"

34

Ava, May 11th, 2015

OKAY, SO THERE'S ARE BABIES UNACCOUNTED FOR. If the twins are, in fact, James's kids, and Lacey wasn't pregnant, then we are missing some babies. Sally walked away from us, presumably to keep her word to Captain Brooks with the update from Matza and the hospital.

While we wait for her to return, I start walking in circles and making a verbal list of possibilities about the baby.

"Could be Lacey looking into an adoption… Did y'all talk about that at all?"

"No, never," James says.

"Hmmm… Maybe she had some oopsie babies in high school! And she was trying to track him or her down?"

"No, she definitely *did not* have any 'oopsie' babies," he says, with an extra emphasis on the 'did not.' "I would have been told about it. Someone would have told me… her family… or a friend. No. She never had a baby before Annie."

"Okay… maybe the call was about someone else's kids. Maybe your mistress is pregnant! Have you thought about that?"

"Christ, Ava, I don't have a mistress and no she isn't," he replies. "Trust me."

His tone annoys me, so I push on.

"James, we have to know who she is. She could be the center of all this, we need to at least check."

"She doesn't matter."

"You know any good detective would consider any and all affairs."

"You're not a detective!"

I stare at James for a long time, until he finally breaks our staring contest and looks down at his feet. I wait him out, partly because I'm being polite, but partly because I have nothing else to say.

"You're going to hate me," he says.

"I promise I won't."

He looks up at the sky, squinting into the hazy sun, and I feel his frustration. "She isn't pregnant, there's no way... it's Marian Davis. Clint's wife," he says. "Please, please keep Clint in the dark. Unless you find something solid against her, please keep him in the dark." My jaw hits the floor.

"MARIAN? No effing way. How did that even happen? Are you sure Clint doesn't know?"

"I don't know. If he does, he's one hell of an actor. Hasn't treated me any differently at all."

"Marian. No kidding... Wow, that will be a fun interview," I say, as Sally walks back and joins us.

"What will be a fun interview? What'd I miss?" Sally asks, looking from me to James.

James continues looking at the sky, refusing to look at Sally and basically pretending we have disappeared. I look to Sally and nod toward the car. "I'll fill you in on the road," I whisper.

We leave James on the sidewalk and I hop in Sally's car, telling her all about Marian and Clint on the way home. I look up the Davis's home number, and wonder how best to approach this.

"Maybe we should call Detective Grimm and let her do the interview. I don't really want Marian to know that I know, especially since I work down the hall from her husband. I can't believe James would do that to Clint and Lacey. He just doesn't seem like the type," I say, shaking my head.

"Every guy is the type," Sally says, "and you're right, we should loop in Grimm."

After a quick conversation with the detective, she agrees to let Sally and I watch from behind the mirror as she interviews Marian. We turn the car around and head south toward the station.

Grimm tucks us away before Marian arrives to ensure she doesn't see me.

"If she walks into the room pregnant, this is going to be an intense interrogation. But if she's pregnant, how could she have over-powered Lacey?" I ask.

"Well," Sally starts.

"I mean," I say, interrupting her, "I guess Lacey was pretty defenseless, being naked and soaking in a tub."

"Right," Sally agrees. "But is Marian a killer?"

"I don't know. I've only met her a few times; she seems sweet, but almost too sweet. It makes me think she's faking it. Wouldn't have Clint mentioned that she was pregnant? Surely he would have."

"You'd think," Sally nods.

"Although, to be honest, Clint and I almost exclusively talk about work, and I can't think of the last time we were chatting at the water cooler about our personal lives."

"Hmmm."

I lean against the glass, tapping my chin with my phone. *Did he mention she was pregnant and I just wasn't listening?*

After another twenty minutes of waiting, we see the door open and both hold our breath as Grimm follows a very pregnant Marian Davis into the room.

35

James, May 11th, 2015

I CONTINUE STARING AT THE SKY UNTIL MY EYES WATER. Even though it's extremely overcast and muggy, the sun is finding a way to keep it annoyingly bright outside. I hear Ava and Sally leave, but my feet are like cement, stuck in place. I'm not sure how long I stand here, but eventually I get too hot to stay any longer, and I finally head to my car. Once inside, I'm not sure what to do. I can't go home or to the hotel — both are still taped off crime scenes. I'm not sure if Ava is mad at me, so I can't decide if it's safe to return to her place. I decide to call Rick, who agrees to meet me for lunch.

It's only ten thirty, giving me an hour to sit and suffer my own thoughts. The incident with Marian was a complete mistake, really ridiculous. I don't even find her attractive, it was just an odd moment of weakness. She was just so willing, and it was late, we were alone. I haven't seen her since; she's never tried to contact me. Clint clearly has no idea, because there's never been any tension in the office. She can't have done this, it just doesn't fit. She's happy with Clint, and he's happy, too.

After what feels like days, Rick walks into the restaurant.

"How are the kids?" he asks me, sliding into the booth.

"Good, I think. We Facetimed earlier today. Annie and the twins seem okay, but your parents are obviously struggling," I tell him. Rick says nothing, so I continue, "As soon as we find her killer, I'm going to stay in Austin for a while. I need to take some time off work, I've saved up some holiday time."

Rick's silence continues because our server arrives; he orders a Greek salad, and I order chicken kabobs.

"I might need somewhere to stay," I say.

"Might?"

"It's complicated."

"Try me," he says.

"Well, someone shot up my hotel room. They stole some photos and all my notes about Lacey."

"Someone tried to shoot you? Why didn't you tell me that?"

"Yeah, I guess they did… I didn't know. I've been…confused. And then I was staying with Ava, but…it didn't feel right," I lie. No point telling him the whole truth, I think.

"Are there any leads on the shooter?"

"I don't know yet. My only lead is Brandon Bennett, do you know him?"

Rick shakes his head.

"He's a doctor in the Cancer Center. Problem is, according to Sally – Ava's aunt, the forensic scientist I was telling you about? She says there's no gun registered to him. I haven't heard yet if the CSU results are in to know if there was anything, DNA, a hair, saliva, whatever, left in the hotel room."

Our food arrives, and we expertly push it around the plate; neither of us is particularly hungry. We try to small talk about other things, but end up sitting mostly in silence. After the table is cleared, we get up to leave.

"Keep me in the loop, will you?" Rick asks me. "And try not to get yourself killed."

36

Ava, May 11th, 2015

SALLY AND I ARE STILL GETTING OVER THE SHOCK OF SEEING MARIAN PREGNANT WHEN GRIMM STARTS HER INTERVIEW.

"Thank you for meeting me, Mrs. Davis, I'm Detective Grimm," she begins.

"Good Morning, Detective," Marian replies, nodding to Grimm, "How can I help you?" She rubs a hand subconsciously across her baby bump and repositions herself in the chair. "Ugh, I'm ready for this baby to come out."

"You're very pregnant; when are you due?" Grimm asks her.

"Next month, June 18th, little girl in here," she responds with a smile.

"Congratulations," Grimm says. "Do you have a name picked out?"

"Elizabeth, after my grandmother. But we're gonna call her Beth."

"Do you have any other children?"

"No, no, little Beth here is our first! We are so excited. Didn't have to try at all, can you believe it? Just decided we were ready one day and BAM! Pregnant the next day."

"Mrs. Davis—"

"Please, hun, call me Marian," she interrupts.

"Okay, Marian, I hate to ask you this, but is there any way this child is James Abbott's?"

Marian laughs a maniacal laugh that sends chills down my spine.

"Heavens, no. Is that what he said? He needs to re-take Sex Ed!"

"Excuse me?"

"What James and I had, good Lord Almighty, it was…well, it was a drunken blow job in his office," she whispers. "Oh, hun, I stumbled in, looking for Clint right? I'd been at a girls' night dinner just up the road. Only Clint had gone home, and I found James instead. He looked sad, lonely, and I sort of flung myself on him. I have no idea why," she adds, "it just seemed like the right way to make him smile. I do funny things like that sometimes. But I'm wholly sworn to Clint, he's the only man I've ever laid in bed with!"

Grimm forces a laugh at this. If James needs to retake Sex Ed, she needs to retake her marriage vows.

* * * * *

After the interview with Marian, I offer to take Sally and Grimm out for lunch. I figure if we are going to work together, we should get to know each other a little better.

"How about Mexican?" Grimm suggests.

"Sounds perfect," I agree.

"TT's Tacos? It's right across the street," Grimm asks, and Sally and I agree. We follow Grimm down the elevator and out the lobby of the police station. From the outside, the station looks like any average 1970s brown brick building. There's a tiny sign above the porte-cochére that says "Dallas Police Department", but it's hardly visible from the sidewalk, let alone the street. Cater-cornered from the station is

TT's, a complete dive that probably has a roach infestation. I shudder slightly at the thought of cricket-filled taco and walk humbly into the restaurant.

"The thing about in-house murders is it's almost always the spouse," Grimm informs us, grabbing a table near the soda fountain — a navy blue booth that's peeling apart. I take a seat across from Grimm and Sally sits down next to me.

"But not always," Sally points out.

"Sure, there are exceptions. Some episode of Dateline must have mentioned that hiding in plain sight is the best alibi, when really it's the worst. If your wife dies in your house, people are going to look at you, not gloss over you. Holding someone down while they take a bubble bath is gruesome, personal, and full of hate. Taking the time to mop up all the splashed water and suds, well, there's no word for that level of contempt," Grimm states.

"James doesn't fit the build, trust me, I know him," I state.

"Fit the bill," Sally corrects.

"Whatever," I reply.

"Maybe he does, maybe he doesn't," Grimm responds, ignoring us, "he could be an excellent actor."

"He isn't."

"Look, I started on the force in patrol, like everyone does, about ten years ago. Nine months into my career, I pulled over a drunk driver who had a dead body in the backseat. I was twenty-two at the time, my first dead body, and I threw up everywhere contaminating the crime scene."

"Just like James did when he saw Lacey," I chime in.

"Yup, just like that," Grimm agrees. She finishes her taco and then continues, "Instead of being fired on the spot, the homicide detectives let me tag along and redeem myself. Determined to prove my worth, I didn't sleep until I solved the case — it took me three days when it should have taken one."

"What happened?"

"The driver's name was Jimmy West, and it was his wife, Christina, in the backseat. He was completely wasted, and claimed not to have noticed the body. We arrested him for a DUI and while he sobered up in a holding cell, we promptly started investigating his wife's murder.

"We were able to create their evening timeline with ease; Mr. and Mrs. West arrived at a bar in Deep Ellum — which was a really sketchy neighborhood at the time — around three o'clock in the afternoon, to watch a Cowboys game. They were regulars, so many of the bartenders and several other patrons recognized them when we came by asking questions. Witnesses saw Mrs. West leave around eight pm. At precisely nine thirty-six pm, Mr. West tabbed out and left the bar. Time of death was determined to be eight fifteen pm.

"The bar's security camera was just for show; we couldn't see what happened between eight o'clock and nine thirty-six, but the assumption was that Christina walked out of the bar, argued with someone, was shot and then crammed into her own backseat. We figured this was to threaten or warn Jimmy. I wasted many hours tracking down everyone that either of them had ever argued with, and then I realized the one thing that was left out of all the witness statements: the reason his wife left early.

"Once I had a hunch that Jimmy was involved, the story unraveled quickly. They had been very loudly arguing for nearly fifteen minutes in the bar, until she slapped him across the face and stormed out. Jimmy ordered a shot of Tito's Vodka, excused himself to the restroom, came back several minutes later and ended up having six additional vodka shots and four PBR's. After that case, I promised myself I would always interrogate the husband first."

"But James is different, surely you think so, too?"

"Ava, all the signs tell me it was James. No sign of forced entry. Nobody heard any screams, or saw any strangers in or near the house. No defensive wounds on the victim, no sign of a struggle. She clearly welcomed the killer into her bathroom, where she was soaking naked. Other than your husband, who do you let see you naked?"

"If you're in a tub and someone walks in, I'd hardly consider that welcoming them in," I argue.

"Yeah, that's more like an unfortunate happening," Sally agrees.

"Look, I've read his file twenty-five times: James Abbott: Age forty. Six foot one, very short brown hair — starting to bald. Principal and top producer at QV Commercial, a large privately held real estate company. Only child with deceased parents — car accident five years ago. Married, three children ages four and one. No criminal record. So what makes a man that doesn't fit the bill, fit the bill?" she asks us.

I look at Sally, who probably has an answer but decides to stay silent.

"I think to myself, okay, it's got to be an affair, or alcohol abuse, or drug use. Maybe a personality disorder, or a mental illness. But his blood alcohol content was zero—he hadn't had a sip of the scotch he poured. No signs of past drug use, and none were found in his system. No medical records of mental illness, at least not diagnosed, no prescriptions in the medicine cabinet with his name on them. So what am I left with? An affair then?" Grimm asks.

"It wasn't Marian," I remind her.

"I'm not talking about Marian," Grimm replies.

37

Courtney

I HEARD JAMES CONFESS TO LACEY ABOUT GETTING A BLOW JOB IN HIS OFFICE. They both must have thought I'd already left, but I was in the kitchen making a cup of coffee to take to-go. He sounded pathetic, weak, it made me so mad at him. I took an extra five minutes stirring my milk and sugar, just so I could keep listening. She didn't cry at all, at least not loud enough for me to hear her. She didn't really say anything and he wouldn't stop talking. It was some bitch he met through work. It meant nothing, he said, nothing. He kept repeating the word 'nothing'. Such a liar. All men lie, but this, this was really bad.

He probably thought it would cleanse his conscience, at least partially, by telling her, but I think they both felt worse after that. Some things are better left unsaid.

38

James, May 11th, 2015

AVA SENT ME A TEXT SAYING MARIAN WAS CLEARED, CLINT DOESN'T KNOW ANYTHING, AND COULD I MEET HER AT HER CONDO? I told her yes and headed that way.

She let me in without a word, and led me into her living room where Sally was there waiting with a smile.

"So," Sally begins, "we hear it was *just a blow job*," and laughs.

Christ. I decide to say nothing, because I can't really think of anything to say.

"We didn't invite you over to tease you about Marian, just wanted to let you know that we know," Ava says, with a glare over in Sally's direction. "With her most likely off the list, we aren't really sure where to turn for the babies. Do you recognize this man?" and she hands me a picture of a very handsome black guy.

"No, should I?" I say.

"This is Dr. Brandon Bennett, Oncologist, practicing at Presbyterian Hospital. We are assuming this was Lacey's lunch date. What do you think?"

"I think I hate him," I reply.

"We've called him five times, straight to voicemail. Sal ran a trace on his phone, but it's either dead or turned off, so we can't be sure he is even at home. Grimm sent an undercover patrol officer to wait outside his house; he's to call her as soon as Brandon or his wife get home, but there's been no activity on the house all day."

"Why don't we just barge in? See if they are hiding in the back?"

"You can't just barge in without a warrant, which we won't get solely on the premise that you hate him for buying your son a teddy bear," Sally snaps at me. "Sorry, that was harsh."

"Anyway," Ava continues, shooting a second evil glare at Sally, "we can't legally barge in. Here's what I'm thinking," she says clearing her throat, "You and I walk up to the house and peek around, see if anything looks suspicious — maybe something has been knocked over or some other visible sign of a struggle. Just a couple of concerned citizens checking in on the neighbors because, I don't know, maybe we heard loud shouting. If we see something, we break in."

"Sounds like a good plan to me," I reply.

"I knew you'd be on board!" Ava cheers. "Sally, what do you think?"

"Does it matter what I think?"

"Not really," Ava replies.

"Great," I say. "Let's go."

39

Ava, May 11th, 2015

I PARK MY HONDA CR-V DOWN THE STREET AND WE SLOWLY WALK UP TO THE BENNETT'S HOUSE. The entire front of the house is covered in windows making it easy to see that nobody is home. Sally walks over to the sedan across the street and distracts the undercover officer while James and I slip around the side of the house.

It only takes us about three minutes to find the master bedroom window. I see a pair of feet sticking out of the closet and lots of dried blood all over the floor. James starts to dry heave; I grab his arm and pull him back around to the front of the house before he can throw up on the property.

"Shit," I say to Sally and the undercover officer. "You can't really see anything from the outside, but you can tell it's not good. A body is in their bedroom all the way at the back, curtains are wide open. There's blood everywhere."

"Y'all really shouldn't have done this," the cop declares.

"Right, and you'd be sitting here in your uncomfortable car all night long with no movement on the house. Consider it a favor," Sally responds. The cop rolls his eyes.

"I'll page Grimm... chalk it up as an anonymous call, I guess," he says, "I can't believe you did this."

"We didn't break in, I don't know why you're so upset," I inform him.

"You hopped over their fence!"

"Minor detail," James retorts.

It takes about an hour for Grimm and Captain Brooks to arrive, but when they do, they have a warrant to enter the premises.

"An anonymous call, huh?" Grimm inquires, eyeing us up and down.

"Lay off 'em, Susie," Brooks orders, gnawing on a toothpick. "Y'all all right?" he asks us.

"Fine, thanks," we reply in unison. We sheepishly follow Grimm and Brooks up the walk, casting devilish smiles at each other. I know we shouldn't have done this, but I can't help feeling like a true detective. After knocking for several minutes with no response, Grimm smashes the glass panel on the front door, reaches in to turn the lock, and walks into the house.

Everything in the front room is as immaculate as if a maid recently cleaned. Through the entry is the kitchen; a sparkling white kitchen straight out of a magazine. There's a baby blue kettle on the stove and fake lilies in a vase on the kitchen island. A small magnet on the fridge reads 'A full belly is a happy belly!' with a little picture of a cherub below it.

Off to the right is a dining table set for six guests, complete with a gold charger, white plate, gold napkin, and white bowl. There's a water goblet, wine glass, and full set of gold silverware at each seat. "If the silverware is gold, do you call it goldware?" I ask the room.

"Who cares?" Sally responds.

"Just wondering, jeez," I bark.

I turn from the dining table and follow Sally to the left through a large archway that opens into the hall corridor. Four bedrooms branch off the hallway, with the master in the back. Grimm and Brooks clear all the rooms before approaching the master. Sally and I tiptoe behind them.

The scene inside the bedroom is one of the weirdest things I've ever seen. The master closet is color coordinated on both the man and woman's side, though the woman's side has been completely replaced and is full of pink and blue baby clothes. The body of Dr. Bennett is face down on the floor of the closet, his face resting on a Hello Kitty backpack and his hand is clutching a tiny army ranger.

The en-suite bathroom is the same all-white color scheme as the kitchen, complete with his and her sinks, a separate tub/shower, and a private commode. All the drawers are full of toiletries; Brandon's side has combs, beard balm, a toothbrush and paste, among other items. His wife's side, like the closet, has been replaced with baby things. Diapers, wipes, rash cream, Vaseline and a bunch of tiny bows.

The bed is made, the end tables are clean, and the curtains are pulled back letting in the light from a pair of French doors that open to the backyard. CSU arrives as we're staring out the window and they start snapping photos and wiping for prints. Sally is in the corner on her laptop, alternating between feverishly typing and reading.

"They don't have any photos anywhere," I point out. "Isn't that weird?"

"Pretty weird, yeah," James agrees.

"What'd you get on the wife?" I ask Sally.

"Jessica Bennett, age thirty-seven. Five ten with long blonde hair, according to her driver's license. She's currently employed by Teton Technology and has been there thirteen years. Her last bank statement shows a May sixth cash withdrawal of five hundred thousand dollars from the Chase branch at Mockingbird and Greenville. Then she wire-transferred their remaining balance to her parents."

"Cell phone?"

"Got her number, last ping off a cell tower was yesterday in Gun Barrel City. She isn't making or receiving many calls."

"Gun Barrel City? What was she doing there?" James asks.

Sally glares at him for a second before saying, "I don't know, James, I'm giving you this information in real time."

"Sorry," he pouts.

"Any bank statements at Buy Buy Baby, Babies' R Us, or Target?" I ask.

"Nope, nothing at Walmart, Carter's, Crew Cuts, or Janie and Jack either. Must have paid cash for the baby gear."

"What does Teton Technology do?" I ask.

"I thought you'd never ask. They manufacture two things: the Teton Digital Thermal Printer, which prints ID cards, and the Teton Transparent Hologram, which is — obviously — the overlay on licenses."

"Oh, obviously," James mocks.

"And she was in charge of?" I ask, ignoring James.

"She's a Printer Technician. She makes sure the equipment works."

"So what you're saying is...she could have created a new ID for herself? She could be anywhere, under any name with a new look?" James asks.

"Plus, she's had a head start on us," I remind them.

"Two days to be exact," the medical examiner chimes in. "Liver temp tells us our doctor died on May tenth."

"Hmmm. She killed Lacey on the night of the eighth, and then she did… what? Hung out for two days, tore through James's hotel room, shot up her husband and is now…where?"

"You find a phone on the body?" Sally asks Grimm.

"Yes," she says and tosses it to her. "Jacket pocket. CSU lifted a partial, running it now."

Sally plugs the phone into her computer and runs all the data. "Okay… we've got the one call to Lacey. The phone GPS pinged off a cell tower by the hospital. And, surprise, surprise, a call to you. I guess he didn't throw it in the Trinity after all." She says to me as she tosses it back to Grimm.

"So *he* gave me the warning about the babies? Why? Where are the babies! This is driving me crazy," I insist.

"How'd he get your number?" Sally asks.

"I don't know. Google? I'm easy to find, I'm a real estate broker."

"Fair point," she says.

"I'm going to grab one of the CSU guys and head to Brandon's office. We will bag everything, *everything*, and bring it to Central Station," Grimm tells us, "Cap says I'm to continue including you in the case, so you can meet me there in two hours and we can go through it together."

Clearly dismissing us from the scene, we say thanks to Grimm and head home to grab a bite and change clothes before meeting her back at the station. We park in front of my building and are greeted by a very flustered Dr. Chung.

"I had to see you right away, I just received this in the mail," Dr. Chung says, and she hands me a letter.

"Why me?" I ask her.

"I didn't know where else to go," she replies.

40

Lacey, Letter to Dr. Chung

Dr. Chung,

I'm sorry I missed our last appointment. I wanted to be there to tell you this story, because I needed someone to hear it, someone who was sure to believe it. But I feared for the life of my kids and decided I couldn't leave them alone with Courtney.

It started a few weeks ago. I noticed a white Lexus SUV following me everywhere. At first I thought I was going crazy, white Lexus SUVs are really common. But then I saw it idling down the street from my house, and I just knew, call it a mother's instinct.

After a few more days, I decided I needed to do something. I asked Courtney to borrow my car and gave her a list of errands to run. She agreed, and headed out. I waited a minute or two, hopped in her car, and followed. The SUV picked us up at the dry cleaners. I noticed it was a woman, and through the windshield she looked beautiful.

After about three hours, my stalker left us at the Post Office. Now it was my turn to be on the tail. She headed straight home, to a gorgeous ranch-style house in Lakewood. I didn't recognize her when she got out of the car, but I was right, she's very pretty. Nearly six feet tall, model legs, long strawberry blonde hair.

I'm not familiar with her house or her block. I'm very sure I've never been there before, and I can't think of a reason this person would be following me. I continued sitting in my car, wondering what the hell is going on, when a black sedan pulled into her driveway, and Brandon climbed out.

I'll spare you the details on how stunned I was. He walked in the front door, and I watched him kiss the woman and collapse onto the couch. Disgusted with the situation, I turned on the car and went home.

I waited until the next day to text Brandon, and he agreed to meet me for a coffee at this place called Grounds. I wasted no time in confronting him. What I didn't expect was the look of shock on his face.

He didn't say anything for a long time, and then all he said is, "She must think it's you." What? I asked him. And then he spilled the entire story.

He has been having an affair with Courtney for the last year and a half. It all started when he stopped by with the gifts for Jacob and Luke. I was exhausted, really out of it, I hardly remember the day. Somehow a connection sparked, and they fell in lust, and ultimately, love. They'd been using our house for their shenanigans, because Courtney has three roommates and no privacy, and he's married so obviously his house was out. He said they called it black-ops, because she'd never been with a black guy before.

A couple of weeks ago, Courtney discovered she was pregnant — which explains the Summer Flu. Brandon is ecstatic. Apparently he and his wife, Jessica — I finally learned her name — had tried to have children for years. They did three rounds of IUI and two rounds of IVF, but nothing worked.

I guess they had decided they would be fine just the two of them, but then he met Courtney. So young, so full of life. And now he finally gets a kid of his own! His eyes lit up for the first time during the entire story. He said that he and Courtney agreed to wait until she was into her thirteenth week before he told Jessica and asked for a divorce.

Clearly, this plan backfired and Jessica discovered something. Whether she knew about the baby, we weren't sure. But she was clearly aware of the affair, and was calculating her next move by stalking me and my children.

After we finished our coffees, I went out and bought one of those pre-paid phones from the mall kiosk and dropped it off at the hospital for Brandon. I hoped he wouldn't need to use it, but I figured his wife was probably monitoring his phone, and that puts both me and Courtney in danger. I told him to only contact us on this phone from now on.

The next day, I got a call from Brandon on the phone. 'She knows about the baby,' he said. I agreed to meet for lunch so he could tell me what happened.

Apparently, she moved all her things out and replaced her closet with baby clothing...crazy, right? He has no idea where she is, and he's concerned, mostly worried for me and my children. 'I can take care of myself, don't worry about that. But you need to be careful, she thinks we were having an affair. Who knows what she is capable of in this state. And if it's not too much to ask, please take care of Courtney, don't let her go home alone,' he said to me.

So you see? I couldn't leave them. But I had to tell you, just in case. Now you officially know everything that I know, and quite a bit more than everyone else involved.

Hopefully, Brandon is able to take care of this situation. But it sounds like his wife has a screw loose, so I'm not going to rely on it. Until this blows over, I'm glued to Courtney and my kids. I've asked Courtney to stay with us for a few days, so I can keep an eye on her.

I told him if anything happens to me, to protect James and my children. But I'm asking you, too. If anything happens…you're the only one who knows. You might talk to James's only friend, Ava O'Neill, she'll be able to help you and, hopefully, him, too.

Lacey

41

Ava, May 11th, 2015

"THE REASON I GOT SO MAD AT JAMES FOR REKINDLING WITH LACEY WAS BECAUSE I WAS AFRAID BRANDON WOULD DO THE SAME TO ME. What we had was so intense, so special, I basically grew around him and couldn't afford to lose him. And then I found out about the baby, and I really couldn't afford — both economically and mentally — for him to leave me. He made me promise not to do anything drastic until I reached thirteen weeks and we knew the baby was healthy. Because I love him, I agreed. But then I did a drop by at the hospital, to surprise him, you know? With one of those cute little onesies that says '*My dad is the BEST dad.*' And *she* was there. I saw him kiss her, his wife, and it was as if he had stabbed me in the belly.

"I frantically drove to my doctor to get an ultra-sound print out," Courtney says, handing me a copy.

I stare at the sonogram for a long time. You can't really see the baby, but it's obviously a sonogram. I hand both Lacey's letter and the photo to James, who makes a disgusted noise.

"Where did you put the photo?" I ask her, ignoring James's grunts.

"In the back pocket of his jeans. He never empties his pockets before taking off his pants. I knew he wouldn't find it, but she would," Courtney says. "I shouldn't have done it, and it was probably overkill for me to write Baby Bennett on the bottom. Obviously, I didn't know she was crazy, or I never would have done it. She meant to kill *me*, you don't think I realize that?"

I think about that for a second. She meant to kill Courtney, who was in the house at the time. So why kill Lacey? Did she do so little research that she didn't actually know what Courtney looks like? Or had she just followed Brandon to Lacey's house so many times, she assumed it had to be Lacey? But then why attack James?

James and I decide to take Courtney, the letter, and the photo with us to the station, and give it all to Grimm to deal with. After a quick interview, Grimm sends Courtney home with an officer to keep an eye on her and her apartment. If Jessica realizes she killed the wrong woman, she might still go after Courtney, which is scary for Courtney, but will help us find Jessica.

Grimm said she would put out a BOLO on Jessica's physical description and on her car, a 2013 white Lexus SUV, but warned me that unlike on tv, BOLOs rarely lead to anything.

After Courtney leaves and is safely at home, we hunker down for a long night of tackling all the documents and boxes retrieved from Brandon's office. James runs out to grab us all a pizza, and I kick off my converse to make myself comfortable as we camp out in the conference room.

We are able to separate everything into two piles: Cancer Patients and Other Information. Turns out Dr. Bennett has a series of secret affairs, and Courtney is just the tip of the iceberg. He had a personal credit card that was exclusively used for hotel rooms and champagne. The transactions date back five years, well before his affair with Courtney began, and continue well after it started.

"Latest hotel bill on the secret credit card is Hyatt House on 75/ NW Highway, reserved on the ninth. James, that's the same day your room was ranshackled," I point out.

"Ransacked," Sally corrects.

"Yeah, whatever. I wonder if the hotel gave Jessica the wrong room number by mistake? She went for you, expecting Brandon," I say.

"If that's true, she's really sloppy. Killed the wrong woman, almost killed the wrong man," Grimm declares.

"Not all murderers are evil geniuses," Sally reminds her, "in fact, most of them are quite stupid, or they wouldn't be killing in the first place."

"Here are a bunch of reports on his fertility. He isn't sterile, he sought out tests from one, two," James shuffles some papers, "six different doctors to be sure. Looks to me like he really wanted a child, and probably resented his wife for being unable to provide him with one."

"Maybe that's why he had so many affairs? He was trying to get someone pregnant?" I ask to the room. "Now that we have found the baby, why does this still not make sense?"

"I have a tiny box here full of medication prescribed to his wife; Zoloft, Prozac, Lexapro, all anti-depressants," Sally reports.

"Why did he have all her medicine in his office?" I ask.

"Was he writing the prescriptions?" James asks.

"Yep, looks that way, these must be refills," Sally answers.

"Okay, so we have an infertile wife, clearly depressed, who presumably snaps and goes on a killing spree. Where would someone in this weakened state hide? And where did all her stuff go? All her clothes, toiletries, shoes, every trace of her was taken from the house, and that isn't just one trip to the car," James points out.

"Maybe she had help? What if we've been looking at this all wrong?" I ask.

"What do you mean?"

"Well, Lacey's murder was hands-on rage. That was probably Jessica, full of anger thinking Lacey was pregnant with Brandon's baby. But Brandon's murder…you'd think she'd want to hurt him, too. Like really hurt him, more than just shoot him in the back when he wasn't even looking."

"He's a forty-five-year-old male. Jessica could have never over-powered him," Sally reminds me.

"Neither Jessica nor Brandon has a gun registered to them, so where did she get the gun?" I ask.

"Ava, this is Texas, they could have borrowed one from a friend," James say, "but I agree, it feels like we're missing something."

"Ok, so a variety of options.

A. Jessica killed both Lacey and Brandon.

B. Jessica and an accomplice killed Lacey and Brandon.

C. The two murders are unrelated or at least performed by different people," Grimm notes, while updating her murder board.

"Did the bullets in Brandon's back match the ones in my hotel room?" James asks Grimm.

"They were 9 mill. bullets, but this time the shooter didn't leave any brass behind. The lab is still processing them to see if they were fired from the same gun."

"I've got something!" Sally declares, opening a new file. "The Bennett's own a house on Cedar Creek Lake. I'd bet anything that's where she's hiding. Gun Barrel City, that's where she is."

"Got an address?" I ask her.

"Sure do! Shall we?"

"Let's go."

42

James, May 12th, 2015

GRIMM WOULDN'T LET ME GO TO CEDAR CREEK WITH THEM, SO I'M ON RICK'S COUCH STARING AT MY PHONE WAITING FOR AN UPDATE. It's just after midnight and they've been gone for three hours now. I haven't heard a peep — I've been checking my phone so frequently that Rick said I look like I have a twitch.

I try to Facetime with Annie, thinking she will be a welcome distraction to my current waiting game, but Rita tells me Annie's been asleep for hours. Apparently, Annie is really bummed that she will be missing her recital, but it's just not safe for her to be in Dallas right now.

I really miss my kids — their faces are so pure, ignorant to the traumas of adulthood. I wish they could stay that way forever, though I know they can't.

I lost my parents five years ago in a car accident. I was thirty-six at the time, married with no kids. The driver of an eighteen-wheeler fell asleep at the wheel and smashed my parents' car into a freeway median. They died instantly on impact, supposedly didn't even feel any pain. Doctors tell you this expecting it to be a consolation, but what about the pain of loss I was feeling? Knowing I would never get to see them again, talk to them again? Lacey was pregnant with Annie, a grandchild they would never meet, and that notion tore me apart.

That's really when I dove into my work. I don't have any siblings and Lacey's parents are healthy and well. I didn't have anyone who truly understood the grief I was experiencing, but as long as I was busy, I was distracted from the pain. I think Lacey related my ramp-up in work hours to parenthood, but really it started months before Annie arrived.

I didn't mean to be an absent dad; I wasn't raised that way. My dad was at every dinner, every football game, hell he coached my little league baseball team. I even went to SMU just so I could continue attending family dinners every Sunday night. He was my idol, they both were. I can't imagine growing up without either of them, and my heart hurts for Annie and the boys for losing their mom so young. It seems so unfair, at least I had thirty-six years to be with my parents. Why do they get less than five?

I get lost in my thoughts remembering Lacey and my parents and thinking of my kids, that I almost don't hear my phone finally start to ring. I snap it up quickly, but am saddened when it isn't Ava.

"James? You know who this is?" the voice tells me. With a chill I respond, "I do."

43

Ava, May 12th, 2015

TWO SQUAD CARS, AND DETECTIVE GRIMM, SALLY AND ME, IN MY CAR, PULL UP TO THE BENNETT'S ADDRESS ON CEDAR CREEK LAKE. It's only an hour from the city, so it's possible Jessica hid out here after killing Lacey and before killing Brandon.

The garage door is open and there's no car in the driveway; we send the squad cars to hide a block away, and I park my Honda a few houses down.

We sprint through the rain to the front door and ring the bell. No answer. We scoot around to the back of the house on the lake side. A few lamps are turned on, but there's no sign of movement in the house. We take a seat on the back porch and stare at the rain filling up the lake.

"Who's going to tell Courtney about Brandon's death?" I ask the detective.

"We told her back at the station. She's not doing well," Grimm says.

"Poor thing," Sally says. Grimm mumbles in agreement.

It's about two hours before a car sloshes into the driveway and the beautiful Jessica Bennett steps onto the pavement. "You've got this all wrong," she shouts into the darkness. "I know you are here, I know everything."

She walks up to the front door, puts a key in the lock, and pushes it open. She snaps on the porch light, turns to the street and says, "Come on in, I've got a story for you."

Grimm, Sally and I all glance at each other, simultaneously nod, and step out of the shadows.

Inside the house, we are offered a seat on a wicker couch with plush cushions. The house is decorated in a lake-style shabby chic — everything is navy and white with anchor accents and only water-related artwork. There's a large bookshelf full of games; I can see Monopoly, Sorry, Scrabble, several decks of cards, an Ouija Board, Chinese Checkers and Parcheesi. The bottom two rows of the bookshelf are stacked with DVD movies, and a basket to the right has old VHS tapes. A huge tv is mounted above a wood-burning fireplace, and the kitchen to our left is built with natural wood cabinets and a white tile countertop. Like their house in Dallas, there are no photos of the Bennetts anywhere.

"*So*," she begins. "*So*. You think I killed Lacey. You're wrong."

I look up at Jessica for the first time, and she is every bit the description Lacey wrote in her letter. "Mrs. Bennett, why were you following Lacey Abbott?" I ask her.

"Because that bitch was sleeping with my husband, and I wanted to see what the hooker looked like."

"No, she wasn't. Lacey never touched your husband."

"Tell that to the sonogram I found in his pocket, or the barista at Grounds Coffee who confirms they were dining together last week, or the thirty-five times I followed him to her house when her husband wasn't home."

"The baby isn't Lacey's, you killed the wrong woman."

"Bull shit. I saw her. I saw *them*. All the time." She folds her arms across her chest.

"Tell us about the baby clothes," Grimm says.

"Ugh, you guys are so stupid," she says. She walks into the kitchen and pops a Keurig cup into the coffee machine. We all sit silently, waiting for her to continue. After her mug is full, she says "I'm doing laundry last week and the photo falls out of Brandon's pocket. I was pissed. The affair I could live with, it would burn out, they always do," she catches my reaction, "ohhh-ho, you think I didn't know about his wandering eye? Please. He broke down just as much as I did when our second round of IVF didn't work."

"And how did you recover?"

"Who says I have?"

"Does your medication help?"

"Some days. But sometimes you can't numb yourself enough," she insists, crossing her arms.

"Did Brandon take any medication?"

"No, never. He found his healing in, ah, physical ways. He's been sleeping around for years. Everyone has their vices, I learned to live with his as he learned to live with mine. You don't understand, you're not married," she jabs, looking at my left hand.

"Tell us about the baby clothes," Grimm repeats.

"Right, I'm getting there. I wasn't about to let *him* leave *me*. He thought he was so damn sneaky. Ha! Joke's on him. I hired a divorce attorney after moving all my stuff out and filling the house with baby things. He hasn't even called me."

"Jessica, he's dead," I state, and I don't believe she doesn't already know this. Grimm glares at me.

"No he isn't, why would you say that?"

"Because he is. Shot twice, in your house."

"No."

I look to Sally and Grimm for help. Sally is smirking and Grimm just rolls her eyes.

"Look, Mrs. Bennett, we're going to have to take you into the station to finish up this little interview," Grimm says. "Squad car is outside to escort you back to Dallas."

We get Jessica into the backseat of the car and circle back into her house. After an hour of opening every drawer, door, cushion and book, we bag everything we think needs a second look and head back to town.

* * * * * *

At the station Sally and I are ushered into the observation room to watch Grimm finish the interview with Jessica. Captain Brooks joins us and takes a seat next to Sally. As always, he's chewing a toothpick.

"She didn't run," I tell Captain Brooks.

"So?" he asks.

"So…her job, her skill set — she could have printed herself a new ID and taken off. Why didn't she?"

Brooks looks at me for a few seconds while slowly chewing on his toothpick. He grabs the end and takes it out of his mouth, then thinks better of it, and starts chewing on it again. Before he can respond, Jessica starts talking.

"TV shows do a bad job at showing how uncomfortable it is to sit in the back of cop cars, especially when you're tall and driving for over an hour. The two officers in the front seat didn't say a word the entire ride. Were they following instructions or are they just boring?" she asks Grimm.

"Why don't you finish telling me about your relationship with Brandon," Grimm says, ignoring her. Jessica sighs deeply.

"I don't know how I got here. Last week everything was great. I made chicken parm for the first time ever and Brandon absolutely loved it. We shared a bottle of wine, watched a movie together and held hands the entire time, like a couple of teenagers," she says with a giggle. "And then the next day, my world turned upside down. Brandon was going to have a baby, something he had always wanted, and our fifteen-year marriage crumbled in an instant."

"Look, I wanted to hurt him, absolutely embarrass him, but kill him? Never. If anyone should die for their sins, it's Lacey, cheating on her own husband and ruining another marriage. Creating a bastard child in her fertile belly. But someone already took care of that for me, bless them."

"I already told you, Lacey wasn't pregnant and never had an affair with your husband, so you need to try again. Why did you kill Lacey? You're pretty calm for someone who recently drowned a woman and shot her own husband. Too much Prozac in your system?"

"Hmph," she snorts while chewing her bottom lip, "not enough."

"How did you get into the Abbott's house?"

"I didn't."

"Pretty brutal way to kill someone," Grimm declares, ignoring Jessica and laying out photos of Lacey. "The average adult can't hold their breath for more than thirty seconds. All you had to do was keep her down long enough for her body to react and try to take a breath, causing her to inhale water. But that didn't work, did it? No, you had to break her nose. Did she slip under all on her own after that?"

"I already told you, I didn't," she says, turning her face away from the images.

"What I can't figure out is, why kill her first? Why wait two whole days to attack James and kill Brandon?"

"Attack James? Did James say I attacked him? I've never even seen him — we've only spoken on the phone."

"You've spoken to him?" Grimm asks.

"Yes, twice. I called several days ago to let him know about the affair."

"When exactly? What day?"

"I don't know, May 6th or 7th maybe?" Jessica says.

"Before Lacey was killed," Grimm says, not as a question but more a statement.

"Sure," Jessica says. Grimm turns around to look at us through the glass. Brooks nods, though Grimm can't see him, and steps out of the room.

"Excuse me for just a second," Grimm says, getting up from her chair. She steps outside and shuts the door behind her.

"James knows Jessica?" I say to Sally.

"That's not good," she replies. "He should have told us that."

"I wonder why he didn't?"

Sally shrugs and chews on her big thumbnail. "Grimm and Brooks aren't going to like this," she says after a while. I can't think of anything to say, so I just sit and stare at Jessica through the window. After a few more minutes, Grimm returns, but Brooks does not.

"Look," Jessica says as Grimm returns to sit in her seat, "I didn't kill Lacey or Brandon. I didn't even know Brandon was dead, and I definitely did not attack James. All I did was buy a bunch of baby shit and plant it at the house, then skip over to my lake house to wait. I thought for sure Brandon would call me, but he didn't. I've been out on Cedar Creek for a week. I didn't do any of this. When can I leave?"

"Let's say I believe you. Who do you think would want to kill Brandon?"

"Ha, how much time do you have?" she asks me. "Look, you say Lacey wasn't pregnant, so maybe start with the woman that is?"

"The woman who's pregnant has been cleared for both murders," Grimm tells her.

"Well shit, any number of women could have wanted him dead, he has a new side piece every week. I don't know the lies he tells them, I only know the ones he tells me. Being a doctor always works on his side. People trust doctors. What's her name?"

"Whose?"

"The woman that's pregnant."

"Can't tell you that."

"Horseshit," she mutters.

"Anything else you'd like to add?" Grimm asks her.

"Yes, check her again."

44

James, May 12th, 2015

JESSICA CALLED ME. I don't know why, but I didn't tell Ava or Detective Grimm. The first call was the day before Lacey was killed. She looked me up and called me at the office to tell me that Lacey was having an affair — but that's all she said. She didn't disclose her identity or give me Brandon's name, she just told me she didn't think I should be the only one in the dark.

I didn't believe her, not for a second. Given what I had just put Lacey through, there was no way she would do that to me, to us. I didn't even ask Lacey about it because I knew Jessica was mistaken.

But then the next day, when Lacey was killed, I doubted myself. Suddenly Jessica's story made sense; was it an affair gone wrong, ending in a violent rage? I felt so many emotions: betrayal, loss, angst, regret. Could I have prevented this? What if I had mentioned it to Lacey, would I have been at home earlier that day, talking to her about all this? Would she have stopped hiding her secrets, and told me about Courtney and the letter she wrote to Dr. Chung?

I honestly don't know why I never mentioned that phone call to Ava, but I guess at first I was still struggling to believe everything. And then we learned of the affair between Brandon and Courtney and it seemed irrelevant.

When I answered the call today, and I heard that voice again, I felt like I might be sick. Suddenly all the dots connected. I knew it was Jessica, I just knew it.

My mind was racing. Am I next on her list? Has she completely snapped after finding out about the baby and is she now going to attack everyone remotely connected? But then she started talking, and the fear in her voice, it isn't what I expected.

"James, I'm so sorry, I'm so, so sorry. I promise you, it wasn't me," she said, "and I know you. I know you wouldn't do this."

"You don't know me," I disagreed.

"Yes, yes I do. I did my research on you. You lost both your parents five years ago, you're a workaholic. You have no idea what your wife does all day, or that she was sneaking a man into your house regularly. I've been following Lacey for weeks. Weeks! It's amazing how preoccupied people can be with themselves. She never even noticed me. You don't know that Jacob's shoulder got dislocated last week during the airplane game. Lacey completely lost it, she couldn't believe she'd hurt him. I followed her right into the hospital, and still she didn't see me. The doctor popped it back into place in two seconds and she was *all ohmygod I can't believe this happened. I'm not going to tell James he will just FREAK OUT.* The doc tried to console her, said it happens all the time with young kids, but she was too distraught to even hear him."

"YOU STAY AWAY FROM ME!" I yelled at her, with so much force I might now be hoarse.

"I can't stay away from you, not now," she calmly stated.

"Stay away from me, and stay away from my family. Cops are coming to arrest you right now for your heinous crimes!"

"They won't find me. I'm not home —"

"At the lake. They are waiting for you at the lake. You're done."

45

Ava, May 12th, 2015

SALLY AND I HEAD TO GE'S BURGERS FOR AN EARLY LUNCH WITH OUR LAPTOPS. It's been a long time since I pulled an all-nighter, but my college days taught me I can survive on no sleep so long as I have burgers, fries and caffeine. GE's is our go-to lunch spot because he always gives us the big corner booth and makes sure we are left alone. We order two cheeseburgers, two cokes, some fries to share, and post up for the afternoon.

"You check Jessica's alibi, I'll go through Brandon's emails," I tell Sally.

Sally found Brandon's personal email account for me and it's full of weeds. He gets over sixty marketing emails from various stores, multiple credit card notices, and several love notes each day. I honestly don't know how he has time to keep up with all these emails, have multiple affairs, and take care of his patients, but he must have learned not to sleep.

Filtering out all the coupons and unrelated messages, I find three current mistresses he's been keeping in a recent rotation. Sally does a quick background check on them and writes the following stats on a scrap of paper:

Jeanne Dupre: twenty-five years old, five feet eight inches, blonde, works for an ad agency as a graphic designer. Speeding ticket in 2012.

Morgan Brian: thirty-one years old, five foot seven, blonde, real estate attorney. No criminal record.

Amanda Hopkins: thirty years old, five foot nine, blonde, realtor. Arrested back in 2006 for drunk and disorderly conduct.

"Well, our boy has a type," I say to Sally, "All the girls he's been with lately look exactly like his wife. Tall, blonde, beautiful. Only difference is that the other three have careers; Courtney is the only student," I say, reading their descriptors.

"What are we working on today, ladies?!" GE asks as he pulls up a chair. GE is seventy-five years old but he looks about sixty. He has a full head of gray hair, a 1970s mustache, and a jagged scar on his right eye. Every time I ask him how he got it, he gives me a different answer. *I was running from the bulls in Spain. I was in a knife fight in Tijuana. Shrapnel to the face during an explosion.* I'm not sure I'll ever know what really happened.

"Two murders: an at-home drowning and a double tap to the back," Sally reports.

"Branching out from your usual banter, eh? No good office space on the market? Nothing new being built I need to plop a burger joint next to?"

"We're helping my coworker; his wife was killed. You know anything about that?"

"Yeah, I heard about the drowning. All over the news, wasn't it?"

"You know anything that wasn't in the news?"

"Nah, my people don't mess with petty familial disputes, you know that."

I nod, because I do know that. GE is very well connected—his legal businesses include a chain of restaurants: GE's Burgers, GE's Steak & Chop, and GE's Fish Market. His illegal pursuits consist of small-arms dealing. They call him Grand Excellency, or GE for short, though his actual name is Roger Vaughn.

I met Roger when I was just eight years old, dining in this very restaurant. It doesn't make any sense that we are close now, or that I ever stepped foot in GE's Burgers since that day, but sometimes things just don't make sense.

I remember it like it was yesterday: I was sipping on a milkshake (GE's milkshakes were my favorite thing back then), a special treat from my parents because I'd just won my first one hundred-meter dash at summer track camp, when it happened. A Giant — at least he seemed like a Giant at the time — ran into the restaurant and shot both of my parents. He was never caught.

That was the first day I really noticed GE; I'd been to his restaurant hundreds of times but was always focused on my milkshake. Right after the incident, before the cops even arrived, he scooped me up, attempted to calm me down and took me to Sally's. And Sally ended up with me permanently.

I was a hard-headed child and became obsessed with their murders. I convinced myself I could solve their case and I made Sally bring me to GE's every weekend so that I could search for clues and interview both the regulars and the staff. I had a determination that burned like a fire—I thought if I found the Giant, they would come back to me. Unfortunately, I was unsuccessful.

Eventually, I eased the pain by telling myself the Giant was a crazy lunatic that was dead in a gutter somewhere. It was explained to me much later that the Giant wasn't the cracked-out psychopath I imagined in my head — it turns out he was in the restaurant that day to kill GE, but got my parents by mistake.

"Why was he after GE?" I had asked Sally.

"Because, honey, GE isn't always a good guy. We like him, and he's good to us, but he has enemies," she said to me. Several years later I learned why that is.

I haven't had a milkshake since that day, but I still return to GE's every weekend. Over time, GE became a substitute father to me, weird as that may be. He even paid for my college tuition at SMU and gave me a large lump sum of money when I graduated. It didn't bring my parents back, but I think it made him feel less guilty.

"I think we can eliminate Courtney as a suspect. I mean, why kill Lacey, her employer? Especially being pregnant, she'll need the money," I say. "And why kill her baby daddy? There's just no motive for Courtney to do it."

"TxDOT cameras are terrible, but I can follow a white SUV from 75/Mockingbird Lane to freeway 175 at Jessica's time of departure, but it'll be impossible to tell if she went all the way to the lake, and even more impossible to tell if she came back. Plus, she could have returned in a different vehicle," Sally says, interrupting me. "As far as her cell phone is concerned, it has only pinged off the Gun Barrel City cell tower in the last seven days. Of course, she could have just left it out there when she came back to town to kill her husband."

"We can also eliminate Morgan Brian, our attorney," I say. "She's been in Las Vegas at the ICSC Conference, giving a seminar and sitting in on several others. Credit card has been used several times on the strip in the last few days."

"What you need to find," GE chimes in, "is the person who hates them both equally. If you can't find that, they aren't related murders."

"But how can they not be related?" I ask him.

"Ava, ask yourself why one of his mistresses would kill Lacey, but not his wife? If there isn't a reason, you need to refocus." He gets up and heads back to his office.

"The man's got a point," Sally says.

We wrap up our lunch, yell a thank-you back to GE, and head back to the station for a recap with Grimm. She doesn't say anything, but the tension in the air is thicker than butter. Brooks has not returned, and I can only assume he's having an uncomfortable conversation somewhere with James.

Even though we agree that his mistresses are unlikely, we decide to bring Jeanne and Amanda in for questioning because according to Grimm, *you can never be too thorough.*

Amanda, our realtor, was at an open house all day on Sunday, clearing her for Brandon's murder. She did admit that they were supposed to meet up on the ninth at The Hyatt House, but that he called last minute and canceled. We show her a photo of Lacey who she claims not to recognize. Her alibi is feeble, she was at home alone catching up on Real Housewives the night of the eighth. She confessed that she's been dating a few guys, and that she knew Brandon was dating around as well. We decide she is an unlikely candidate, but Grimm asks her not to leave town in case we have more questions.

"Strike two," Sally says.

"Who's next?" I ask.

"Jeanne Dupre," Grimm says. "She's in Room Three." We follow Grimm into the next interrogation room where Jeanne is sobbing hysterically.

"I have been so mad at him. He never goes this many days without checking in on me, I should have known something was wrong. He wouldn't just stop calling and emailing, we were in love," she says as we take a seat across the table. "We were going to start a family."

"What?" I blurt out.

"I'm pregnant, only eight weeks along. But it's something we both wanted," she cries. "What will I do now?"

"Did you know he was married?" Grimm asks, handing Jeanne a tissue and taking a seat at the table.

"Of course I knew he was married! Why do you think we always rendezvous at my place? Or occasionally in hotels? But his wife was a pill-popping drag, he couldn't stand her. He was going to leave her so we could truly be together, but he wanted to make sure she wouldn't hurt herself. He was helping her get into a good mental place."

"How sweet," Grimm scoffs.

* * * * * *

"Well, at least now we have solved the riddle of the babies," I say.

"You gotta give the guy credit," Sally says to me after the interview with Jeanne, "he's got stamina. To keep five women satisfied, and still have the energy to work in a hospital? I'm impressed."

"You're disgusting," I snarl at her, and we both laugh.

Back at the murder board, Grimm updates our prospects. Grimm erases 'cleared' from James's name and replaces it with 'questioning.' Sally and I chance a glance at each other but don't say anything. The rest of the list reads:

Courtney – Unlikely (no motive) but monitoring

Jessica – Likely, motive for both murders, monitoring

Amanda – Unlikely, though alibi not verifiable for Lacey

Jeanne – Unlikely (no motive), alibi for Lacey

Other Connections??? She writes, followed by several question marks.

"What about the hospital?" Sally asks.

"What, you think Vivian did it?" I say.

"I'm just saying, that's Lacey's and Brandon's connection to each other. Someone signed her in. Was that because she asked them to, or because our murderer was covering their own tracks in some way? GE said to find someone who hates them both. Could be Vivian, I mean why couldn't she make it in on Friday? Or it could be a nurse or a doctor."

"Or maybe a patient?" Grimm asks.

46

James, May 12th, 2015

BEING ALONE, OUT OF THE LOOP, SIDELINED ON RICK'S COUCH IS A SMALL VERSION OF TORTURE. I feel more useless right now than I ever have. I should be out there, hunting down leads, getting us closer to Lacey's killer. I shouldn't be kept in the dark, isolated like this.

I get up off the couch and start pacing the living room. I walk probably three thousand steps around Rick's coffee table before a knock on the door startles me. Peeking through the peephole I see Captain Brooks standing on the front door step. He looks stern, unhappy. *Uh oh…* I think to myself.

"Hey, Brooks," I say, opening the door. "Did you find Jessica?"

"We did," he responds, stepping over the threshold and inviting himself in. "She's interesting. Had a lot to say."

"Did she? That's…good," I reply. I close the door and follow him into the living room.

"It's not good for you. You lied to us," he declares.

"No, I didn't."

"James. You knew her. She told you about the affair. Last week you didn't know Brandon was sleeping with Courtney, you had every reason to believe it was Lacey."

"Brooks," I begin, holding up my hands. "Listen."

"No, James, you listen. Do you realize what we are dealing with here? We drive hours to pick up a suspect, and she tells us that she knows you. That she has talked to you not once, but twice. That you gave her a heads-up we were coming to the lake. Gave her an opportunity to *run*. Why would you do that? Guilt? Do you feel guilty because you killed her husband? Did you want to give her a chance to get away, so she wouldn't be wrongly accused?"

"No!" I shout. "No," I repeat, softly this time. "I feel guilty that I was a bad husband. I feel guilty that I couldn't save Lacey. But don't you stand here and accuse me of murder. I feel no guilt for Jessica. I don't even know her. For all I know, *she* killed my wife. She is the crazy one who ruined everything!"

"She may have ruined nothing."

"What do you mean?"

"I have known Sally for nearly thirty years," Brooks says, ignoring my question. "I wanted to believe you because Sally believes you. I've been lenient with you, when I shouldn't have been. I should have pushed you harder. Omitting information is just as bad as lying, you realize that don't you? I could slap cuffs on you right now."

"Yes, and I'm sorry. I don't know why I didn't tell you. It was a mistake. I just got caught up with everything else and it didn't seem to matter! But Jessica calling me twice doesn't prove I did anything," I insist. Brooks doesn't respond. "Please, please. I swear I didn't do this. You know I didn't. I know you know I didn't."

Brooks stares at me for a long time. His expression is hard to read. After a few seconds he grabs a toothpick out of his pocket and pops it into his mouth. "We'll see," he finally says.

47

Ava, May 12th, 2015

"I'LL REQUEST THE HOSPITAL'S ATTENDING LOGS, SEE WHO WORKS FRIDAYS, WHO WAS IN LAST WEEKEND, OR WHO WASN'T BUT SHOULD HAVE BEEN," GRIMM SAYS. She gets up from the conference room table and heads for the door.

"Can you bring back some coffee?" I ask.

"Sure," Grimm replies. She snaps the door shut and the blinds flutter slightly.

"Great, I'll check Brandon's patient files and start running background checks," Sally says with a yawn.

"What can I do?" I ask. Sally throws me a stack of patient files.

"Read these," she suggests.

"What am I looking at here?"

"Those are the patients he's lost in the last two years. Start with the more recent ones and work backwards."

We hunker down with our new line of prospects, a list that seems to be endless. The rain continues to pour outside, making it even harder to stay awake. Grimm comes back in with a large pot of coffee, three cups, sugar and milk. We all pour a cup, kick off our shoes, and dive in.

After a few minutes, Grimm nearly screams, "I've got something! Allie Martinez, nurse at Presbyterian's Cancer Center. She usually works every Friday, but didn't show up on the eighth and her brother has called her in sick all week," she says as she hands me a post-it with her address.

"Is that abnormal?" I ask.

"She doesn't have a brother," Grimm responds.

I grab my sneakers and we bolt out the door, practically running down the stairs to the parking garage. Sally snags shotgun and I grumble slightly to myself as I climb into the backseat. Grimm starts the Jeep and Uptown Funk by Bruno Mars blares out of the speakers.

"Whoa — sorry," Grimm apologizes. She turns down the music so it's barely audible.

"Jamming on your way to work today?" Sally asks.

"More like drowning out my thoughts," she replies. She taps on the steering wheel to the beat of the music and I see Sally's head slightly bopping. Despite the rain, we hit every green light and reach our destination in less than twenty minutes.

Allie Martinez lives in Lake Highlands, a very nice neighborhood close to the hospital. We park right out front and the first thing I notice is her overflowing mailbox. But then we get out of the car and I see one of her rocking chairs is knocked sideways and her front door knob has about eight promotional flyers tied to it.

"I think we're too late," I say to no one in particular.

"Could be that she's just out of town," Sally says with a fake optimism.

"How has nobody called in a missing person? It looks like she has a week's worth of mail spilling out of her mailbox." I say.

"I'll call for back-up," Grimm declares.

Sally and I follow Grimm across the street and we all walk slowly up to the house, unsure what we are about to find.

The front door's glass insert is covered in a silver film and the blinds on the front windows are closed, making it impossible to see inside. We dodge a few puddles as we walk around the side to the wooden gate in Allie's fence. It's unlocked; we walk right through into the back yard. Her back door is ajar and the door knob is busted off. Grimm loudly announces herself as she taps it open with her foot and steps inside the house.

Sally and I follow her in, walking right into a large living room and are nearly knocked over backwards by the smell. The couch is in place facing the tv, which is tuned to E! network and currently airing one of the Kardashian shows. The lamps from both end tables are smashed into pieces on the floor and the armchair is flipped on its back.

To the right of the living room is the dining room, which seemed to be left out of the fight. A wooden table has a bench on one side and chairs around the other three, all standing up, all pushed in properly. The kitchen opens into the dining room and is decently clean except for a few crusty dishes in the sink. I notice a knife missing from the wood block by the stove, but until we inspect the rest of the kitchen I'm not sure it isn't just misplaced.

Across the living room to the left, we pass an office and enter the wing of bedrooms. Allie's body is face up in the first room; she didn't make it very far. Sally and Grimm check the other bedrooms as I crouch down with her body.

She has bruises on her wrists and face, a few minor cuts and abrasions, and a very serious stab wound in her heart. I try to picture the scene: Allie sitting on her couch as the intruder kicks in the back door, she jumps up, runs around the living room knocking over the lamps and cutting herself on the broken glass. Perhaps she pushed the chair over to try to trip her assailant, or maybe he hopped over it, ultimately knocking it down while running across the living room. This first bedroom is closer than the front door, and I see it does have a lock, but she clearly didn't have enough time to close herself in. The bruising on her wrists tells me she was tightly grabbed but put up a fight. On tv, cops are always able to find DNA under victims' fingernails, and I wonder if that'll be possible here.

I step outside for a quick second to take a deep breath of fresh air while we wait for the Medical Examiner. Further inspection of the house tells us that the office was really just for show, all the drawers in the desk are empty and the built-ins are full of Home Goods knick-knacks and DVDs. The master bedroom has only women's clothing and bath products, verifying that Allie lived here alone. The kitchen gives us our only obvious clue, the murder weapon is an eight-inch chef's knife — our killer left it dirty and bloody in the dishwasher as a gift.

While CSU sweeps for additional evidence, Grimm, Sally and I sit outside going over everything we've learned.

"We have three dead bodies and three different causes of death. All seemingly related because of their work at the hospital," Sally concludes.

"I think our killer was hoping to throw us off by using different methods of murder," I add. "Don't most killers stick to one MO, a calling card of sorts, because they have perfected it and continue to get away with it? Maybe our murderer was hoping to confuse the police into investigating each murder as a separate incident? Or, maybe he thought different police districts would investigate each one because they occurred in different neighborhoods? But we've already bested him, because we know they are connected through the hospital," I declare, feeling like quite the detective. "So now we just need to figure out who would — well it's so obvious, that's it," I announce, while slapping myself in the forehead.

"What's it?" Sally asks me.

"The patient files you gave me. It's the only answer. Our killer has to be one of their patients. Someone dying of cancer, angry they aren't getting better."

"Our killer thinks if he can't live, they shouldn't either?" Grimm asks. "I like it. We'll make a detective of you yet, Ava O'Neill."

"Detective," one of the CSU agents interrupts. "We got something."

"What?" Grimm asks.

"Prints. Several."

"Get a match?"

"Uh-huh," he says, with a sly grin.

"Whose?" I ask.

"James Abbott."

48

Ava, May 12th, 2015

I FEEL MY HEART BEATING AND MY EYES BLINKING, BUT THERE'S NO WAY THIS IS REAL. I'm dreaming, I have to be. I shake my head and try to clear my vision, but everything has turned into shapes. Sally's voice is somewhere nearby, but I can't make out what she's saying.

"Ava," someone says, shaking me. "Hello? Can you hear me?"

"Huh?" I respond, turning my head slightly to the right. "What?"

"Ava," Grimm repeats, and I realize she's snapping her fingers in front of my face. "Hello?"

"Grimm, hey. Sorry," I apologize. "Blacked out for a second."

"You going to be okay?" she asks me.

"Yeah, sure, of course. I'm a professional."

"Not at this," Sally reminds me.

"There's got to be a reason James was here, other than to kill Allie Martinez. There has to be," I insist, regaining my composure.

"I think it might be time for y'all to go home. You're too close to this."

"You really think he did it?" I ask her.

"I don't know, but I have to look into this with the mindset that he may have."

"Why? Isn't it innocent until proven guilty?" I demand. "Haven't you gotten to know him at all!"

"Ava," Sally interrupts, placing her hand on my arm.

"No," I insist, shrugging her off. "No."

"Look," Grimm points out. "There might be a completely normal reason for his prints to be at her house. But there might not, and you are not prepared to handle that. Go home."

"I will not go home!" I shout. I stamp my foot in a childlike manner and for a split second I'm ashamed at my behavior. But it's instantly gone when Sally says she won't leave either.

"Fine, but stay out here and out of my way," Grimm snaps.

Sally and I plop down on the curb, and I rest my chin on my hands. The rain continues to drizzle down on us, but I don't care. Sally puts her arm around me and holds me close, as she used to do when I was a small girl.

I look up and down the street; it's a block of cute, redbrick, ranch-style houses. There's nobody outside, but I see curtains flapping in all the front windows — the neighbors must be wondering why their street is suddenly full of cop cars. Surprisingly, nobody has walked over to ask what happened.

Sally kicks at a rock and watches it bounce into the gutter across the road. "He cheated on Lacey, has spoken several times to Jessica, and somehow knows Allie," she says. "Maybe, just maybe, he isn't the guy we thought we knew."

"Not you too," I decry.

"I'm just saying, it doesn't look good. Grimm is right, you need to be prepared for the worst."

49

Ava, May 12th, 2015

JAMES AND I HAVE BEEN COWORKERS FOR A LONG TIME — MOST OF MY ADULT LIFE ACTUALLY — AND WE WORK EXTREMELY WELL TOGETHER. He's organized, methodical, and fun. He tells a joke on every office tour; goofy dad-jokes he gets from Laffy Taffy candies. It's his thing, always has been. Fun James. He's Fun James.

The only time I've ever seen him get upset was four years ago. We were working on a 100,000 square foot deal that was going to change the tune for us on this one office project. The broker running the deal kept hinting that we had it, and we felt very confident moving through each round of the negotiation. Then, out of nowhere, we were fired off the project. The landlord, our client, decided the deal was taking too long and thought we had made it up to kill time. Six months later, after our Protected List timeframe expired, the new leasing team finished and signed the deal we had been working on. James absolutely lost it.

I remember being surprised watching him melt down. We'd had terrible things happen to us before, but James was always the one to take the high road — to be fair, it was a $500,000 commission that was stolen from us — but still, it was unlike James. His tantrum didn't help us get the money and he singlehandedly confirmed that we'd never get hired by that landlord again when he mailed the asset manager a package of glitter. This might not seem altogether rude, but glitter gets *everywhere*. It's actually a genius way to truly ruin someone's day.

I didn't see James at work for several days after the glitter incident. I think he was embarrassed at his behavior, but I thought it was hilarious. When he did finally come back to work, he pretended the entire thing never happened and we silently agreed never to speak of it.

Outside of that episode, James has never so much as raised his voice. He is not a murderer. No way.

Despite the fact that I was told not to contact James, I call him about ten times. He doesn't pick up, so I text him twice, just asking where he is. His sudden absence isn't making me feel any better. "Where is he?" I ask Sally.

"I don't know," she says with a shrug. I know she doesn't, how could she, but I'm annoyed with her anyway.

Grimm comes back out of the house to give us an update. "His prints are on the front and back doorknobs," she informs us.

"But not the knife?" I ask.

"Not the knife," she confirms.

"See, it wasn't him!"

"We don't know that," she responds. "There aren't any prints on the knife. He may have wiped it clean and forgot to wipe the doors."

"Who wouldn't wipe down everything before they left?" I demand.

"An idiot?" Sally inquires.

"Brooks is going to circle back and pick James up. I'm going back to the station, you are going home."

"Brooks would let us stay," I point out.

"No, he wouldn't. Sally can call and ask him if you need proof," Grimm retorts.

"Ava, it's fine. Let's go home, okay?" Sally encourages.

"Fine."

50

Ava, May 12th, 2015

SALLY AND I GRAB AN UBER BACK TO HER PLACE AND SALLY ORDERS US A PIZZA. I'm not particularly hungry, but I pretend to enjoy a slice because I don't want to be rude. James never called me back, but I imagine Grimm has probably taken his phone away by now.

"Want to watch *You've Got Mail*?" Sally asks me after we eat. Somehow, she eats four pieces of pizza. Maybe she's become a nervous eater.

"Sure," I reply dully, throwing my paper plate and uneaten pizza in the trash. I kick the pantry door shut and hop up to sit on the kitchen counter. Sally leans against the cabinets, spinning a straw through her fingers.

"You're not going to take in a word of the movie, are you?" she asks.

"Nope," I respond.

"What do you want to do?"

"I want to know why James was at Allie's house. I don't want to be kicked out of the case, this close to the finish line." Sally flips on the news, and we are hit with large image of James's face. "Hey, turn it up," I insist.

Kailey Harris is back on the story, this time pitching a new angle: "This just in, James Abbott, the *Highland Park Widower* may in fact be our very first *Highland Park Serial Killer*. New evidence ties him to the murders of Presbyterian Oncologist Dr. Brandon Bennett and Nurse Practitioner Allie Martinez. More to come tonight at five o'clock."

"Ugh turn that off," I demand. The doorbell rings and Rufus comes trotting into the kitchen. "Are you expecting someone?" I ask.

"No," she replies. We walk over to the door and see Detective Grimm and Captain Brooks through the window. "Hey," she greets them, opening the door. "What's up?"

"Where's James?" Grimm asks.

"What?" I ask.

"Brooks went to pick him up and he wasn't there. His phone was though, and you had called him ten times."

"He didn't answer," I defend myself.

"I told you not to call him," Grimm grates.

"I know," I reply.

"If you want to work with the police, you have to listen to orders, Ava," Brooks explains. "Surely Sally told you that?"

"She did," I agree, looking over at Sally. "I just wasn't listening."

"Any idea where James would go?"

"Did you check his house?"

"We've checked his house, office, Rick's place and his hotel room. He isn't anywhere."

"Well he's somewhere," I retort.

"Don't be a smartass," Sally scolds.

"Sorry," I mumble.

"You know him best. Where would he go?"

"Are you officially asking me for help?" I ask.

Grimm takes a deep breath before responding, "Yes."

"And if I help you, do you promise not to kick me out again?"

Grimm turns to Brooks for an answer. "Yes," he responds. "As long as you promise not to disobey a direct order again."

"Deal," I agree, holding out my hand. Brooks takes it.

"Okay, so if I were James, I'd be running," I declare. I walk into the living room and feel everyone following me. Sally closes the door and turns the lock.

"Away?" Grimm asks.

"No, no, running. Physically. I do my best thinking when my blood is flowing."

"But you're not James," Grimm points out.

"Right, but I know when he does his best thinking."

"Okay…?" Sally encourages.

"Brooks," I begin, pointing to him, "you said you saw him earlier today. Everyone was obviously surprised he knew Jessica, safe to assume you were jammering him about that?"

"Hammering," Sally corrects.

"Whatever, hammering then?" I ask. Brooks nods in agreement. I start pacing in front of them. "That's what I thought. He is probably a little worked up. Let's look at the facts," I suggest: "his wife was murdered, his wife's coworker was murdered, and you put some pressure on him today. His kids are in Austin, his parents are dead, and he has no other family. James is a talker. You should see him at work. He wants to talk everything out. So where does he go to do that?"

"I thought you were going to tell us that," Sally replies.

"I am, I was just looking to see if you guys would guess," I explain. Nobody guesses. "If he's not at Rick's place, he's at my place. I'd bet you anything he's at my place."

"And that is?" Grimm asks.

"Just two blocks away."

51

James, May 12th, 2015

I THINK BROOKS BELIEVES ME, BUT I CAN'T BE SURE. His steely glare is impossible to read, but he doesn't arrest me or drag me back to the station; I'm safe for at least another day.

I pack a small bag and head over to Ava's. She isn't here, but she'll come back eventually, and I can't imagine she'd mind if I make myself comfortable. I take a quick shower and lay down for a nap.

"James?" someone calls from the kitchen, waking me up from a deep sleep. I look over at the clock on the wall and see that I've been napping for three hours.

"In here," I call out. Ava, Sally, Brooks and Grimm all walk into the guest bedroom. "Oh jeez, I wasn't expecting all of you."

"I guess you do know him pretty well," Grimm agrees.

"Are you okay?" Ava asks.

"Yeah, I just needed some rest and Rick's place felt…cold," I reply.

"Well you're always welcome here," she insists.

"Why'd you leave your phone?" Grimm asks, waving my phone in front of my face.

"I forgot it," I reply, grabbing it from her.

"We've been looking for you," Grimm tells me, snatching it back.

"Well, you found me. What are you mad at me for now?"

"How do you know Allie Martinez?" she asks.

"Who?"

"Allie Martinez," she repeats. She grabs a photo out of her purse and hands it to me.

"I don't know her," I reply. I hand her back the photo and climb out of the bed. Standing at eye level, I feel less threatened.

"Then why were you at her house?" Brooks asks.

"When was I at her house?"

"We don't know exactly."

"I'm confused," I admit. "Am I in trouble?"

"Your fingerprints were found in several places in her home," Ava informs me. "Just tell us why you were there."

"What? I wasn't! I don't even know her."

"James," Ava says. "Please help us."

"I'm trying! I swear, I don't know her."

"Then how do you explain the prints?" Grimm asks.

"I don't know. Where does she live anyway?"

"Lake Highlands."

"Lake Highlands?" I ask, "The only people I know in Lake Highlands are the Nowaks," I say, sitting down on the bed. "Is she dead?"

"She is," Grimm informs me.

"Dang. I'm sorry."

"James, if you don't know her, why were you at her house?" Ava asks.

"I wasn't! I told you. I haven't even been to the Nowak's house in months, I haven't been anywhere near Lake Highlands since — oh. Lake Highlands... Oh my god," I declare, slapping my forehead.

"What?" Sally asks.

"I'm being framed," I insist. I look up at Brooks and see him leaning against the dresser. He continues to stare at me, completely expressionless. "Lake Highlands...that explains it. Roanoke Road, right?" I ask him.

"So you do know who she is," Grimm says. Brooks says nothing.

"No, no I don't, I swear. I got a call the other day at work for a prospective new tenant, calling about one of our listings on the Tollway," I explain.

"So?"

"It was weird, but we get weird calls all the time. Our phone numbers are listed on leasing signs all over the city, right, so people call asking for all kinds of things. We have this one building on the Tollway, it's called Tollway Place, and is in no way affiliated with the Tollway Authority or NTTA. Anyway, I get about fifteen calls a day from people asking me if they can place a toll-tag order. Another one of our buildings has Sympathy Care signage on it? You know the building I'm talking about? In east Plano? The calls I get off that sign... Sheesh. What I'm saying is, I'm used to getting weird calls."

"Get to the point, James," Sally nudges.

"Oh, right, yeah. So anyway, this guy called me the other day and said he had a client who was interested in leasing space, and he asked me if it would be too much trouble if I dropped off our building information. He was looking for a full floor, which is 40,000 square feet in that building. That's a big deal."

"You didn't tell me this," Ava says.

"Yes, well, you weren't in the office at the time and then everything happened with Lacey... It slipped my mind," I explain.

"But you went to his house? Didn't you think that was creepy?"

"Well sure, odd at least, but he said he had just moved here to start his own company and was working from home until he found the right office space for his shop. I tried to pitch our Central Expressway product, you know, to be close to his house. He said he'd schedule a time to come tour it."

"Right," Ava says, rolling her eyes.

"Right. Anyway. The guy said he needed the materials for a big meeting he had in the morning and would it be okay if I stopped by? His printer wasn't working. I'm a grown man and it was the middle of the day, at no point did it cross my mind I'd be in danger."

"What happened once you got there?"

"He had left a note on the front door telling me to come on in and head out to the back yard. I did, and he had a guy there repairing his fence. His story seemed legit. I told him about the building, gave him some floor plans, pricing, and a brochure. He asked a few questions about the rental rate and operating expenses, we shook hands and I left."

"He allured you there to leave your prints on the doors," Ava insists.

"Lured," Sally corrects her. Ava sighs.

"What was his name?" Grimm asks, ignoring them both.

"I don't remember, Jim maybe? He probably gave me a fake name anyway. He didn't give me a card."

"He called you though, right?" Ava asks.

"Yeah! At my office. We can find him through his phone number, right?" I ask.

"Should be able to," Grimm replies.

"I can do it," Sally volunteers. "Give me ten minutes."

"Sally, we should probably take care of this," Grimm tells her.

"Yeah, go right ahead. You'll get the answer next week, and I'll get it in a few minutes. Be right back," she says as she walks out the door.

"Where is she going?" Grimm asks.

"I think she's going to her lab… She can do a lot from there."

"Cool," I agree. Grimm rolls her eyes and Ava walks into the kitchen and pours herself a glass of water. Grimm and Brooks follow her out of the bedroom, and I sneak into the bathroom to brush my teeth.

"I like your place," I hear Grimm tell Ava.

"Thanks," Ava replies. "Where do you live?"

"East Dallas," Grimm responds. "Nothing this fancy." When I walk out of the bedroom, all three of them are sitting in the living room.

"Can I get you guys anything?" Ava asks, a little awkwardly.

"No, thanks," Brooks replies. "On the clock. Otherwise I'd be interested in the kegerator you have back there."

"It was a burner!" Sally exclaims, blowing through the front door in a very Kramer-esque way.

"That was quick!" Ava responds, sounding relieved.

"No way to trace that phone back to anyone. Need to try a different tactic."

"Have we ruled out a patient relation?" Ava asks.

"No," Grimm answers.

"Might still be able to find him that way?"

"Might be our only way," Sally points out.

"Let's go," Grimm suggests.

"Can I come?" I ask. Grimm looks to Brooks, who slowly nods his head.

"Yes, consider yourself under surveillance," Brooks commands. We head back to the station and divide up Brandon's patient files, searching for those that had Allie as their attending nurse. Six patients fit the bill, but five of them are under 24/7 care at the hospital. We start with the one that isn't: Kent Cordes.

52

James, May 12th, 2015

KENT CORDES IS SIXTY-FIVE YEARS OLD, STAGE ONE PANCREATIC CANCER. They caught it early during a routine physical examination and promptly removed the tumor. He had to undergo one round of chemotherapy anyway, just as a safety precaution.

He lives in Highland Park, about six blocks away from my house. I can't remember Lacey ever mentioning him, but she rarely talked about her patients with me. Occasionally she would open up about someone they lost, and how hard it was for their team to tell the families. She would crawl into bed crying on those days, and I would hold her and tell her everything would be all right — at least she was there to make their last moments comfortable. Then I'd tactfully ask her about the patients that were getting better. She'd light up then and tell me an uplifting story about someone still fighting their cancer.

These moments were hard on us, but also enlightening. Some days I'd come home in a bad mood because a deal I'd been working on blew up, and I'd be reminded that there are worse things happening all around us. Everyone's job is stressful in its own way, I truly believe that, but for me to lose sleep because a tenant's construction cost came in ten dollars a square foot over budget, well, that's just plain idiotic. A few days later I'd have moved on to the next deal and not even remember why I was panicking about the last one. But these patients and their families, they will never forget about the stress of each doctor visit, the pain of each surgery and treatment, the loss of a loved one. I realize now that I relied on Lacey's stories to help me center my own stresses, and I am slightly ashamed to admit it.

I snap out of my thoughts and look over at Ava. She is on the phone digging up more information on Kent, and I catch myself really staring at her. Which pain is worse, I wonder: the pain of loss, or the pain of wonder? Ava never told me about her parents; Sally filled me in yesterday and then everything made sense. Her determination to help me find Lacey's murderer, to keep me from the pain of not knowing, to feel like she is smart enough to solve a case. Now I finally understand.

Within a few minutes Ava hangs up the phone and turns to address me, Grimm, Brooks and Sally.

"Okay, Kent Cordes was released from Presby on May second. His son flew in on the third, helped him pack a few bags and drove him to California. They have been staying in San Diego at the son's house for the last several weeks. The plan is for Kent to permanently move there so the son can keep an eye on him."

"Ugh. Not helpful. What else do we know?" Sally asks the room.

"Ballistics came back, the bullets found in Dr. Bennett's back were fired from the same gun that shot up your hotel room," Grimm informs us.

"Am I a target then?" I ask her.

"It would appear so, but there haven't been any other attempts on your life, which seems odd."

"Maybe that was a delusion," Ava offers, "to make us think the hospital isn't the connection?"

"Diversion," Sally corrects.

"Whatever," Ava says.

"Pretty weak diversion," I say.

"Unless you had died," Grimm says.

"Touché."

"I have a thought," Ava announces. "What if it isn't a patient like I previously thought, but the relative of a patient?"

"What do you know?" Grimm asks.

"Well, when I was reading the deceased patient files earlier, one of them stuck out. Listen to this," she explains, grabbing for the file, "Mr. Chase Carter died two weeks ago, and apparently his son had to be escorted out of the ward. He was screaming that it was all their fault and that *they would pay.* He didn't specify exactly *who* would pay, but his physician was Dr. Bennett, attending nurse was Allie Martinez and there's a note in Mr. Carter's file that says *If he won't take his medicine, call Lacey Abbott.* Seems a little suspicious right?"

Sally grabs the file from Ava, reading through everything she just said. She looks up at Grimm, who nods and says, "On it!" and circles back to her computer.

"Ava, this is it. You've found him!"

53

Ava, May 12th, 2015

CHASE CARTER DIED ON APRIL THIRTIETH OF LUNG CANCER, THOUGH IT HAD RAPIDLY SPREAD AND INFECTED HIS LYMPH NODES, LIVER AND PART OF HIS BRAIN. His funeral was two days later, May second, giving his son, Christopher Carter, less than a week to track down his three targets and put his plan in motion.

Time of death came back on Allie, and she was actually our first victim. She was murdered on May seventh, the day before Lacey. We were able to match his DNA from under her fingernails — I guess tv shows don't have it all wrong. Christopher must have been a rough teenager because he was in the system from a 2008 attack on a 7-Eleven employee.

I can't help but wonder if the cops had found Allie first, could they have caught him fast enough to keep Lacey and Brandon alive? It's unfair to think like this, because there's just no way of knowing, but I can't help myself. Allie lived alone.

I shake my head, thinking how unfair it is that Allie lay dead for five days without anyone calling in a missing person. I remind myself that I live alone; how long would it be before someone noticed I was missing?

"Half a day, Ava," Sally says.

"Hm?"

"I know what you're doing. I talk to you every day. I *see* you almost every day. There is no universe in which you're dead for a week and nobody notices you're missing."

I look up and smile at her, because that's exactly what I needed to hear, and yet it is no consolation on how I feel for Allie. Lacey would have noticed Allie was missing, I think to myself. She would have noticed.

"Here's your warrant!" Captain Brooks says as he hands Grimm a piece of paper. "Two teams are geared up and ready to go with you."

Grimm thanks him, grabs her backup weapon and puts it in an ankle holster, folds the warrant into her back pocket and we all head out the door.

Christopher Carter lives in Mesquite, just east of the city. He lives on a very cute block, though his house is in complete disarray. Vines have completely taken over the property, creeping all over the house and the large tree in the front yard. You almost can't even tell a house exists on the lot, save for a bright red door that peeks out from behind the bushes. Broken pieces of lawn furniture are scattered in the flower bed, and his 2004 Toyota Camry is parked in the gravel driveway with a flat tire.

Grimm sends one team around to the back alley and the other stays with us. As we get out of the car we hear a loud crash inside. Grimm storms through the front door and into the foyer.

"Christopher Carter!" Grimm yells while crossing the threshold. "This is Detective Susie Grimm, we have a warrant for your arrest." She takes another step and WHAM she's knocked forcibly over into the wall, cracking her head on an archway.

As I see her shaking the stars out of her eyes, I look for her assailant. James grabs Christopher and flattens him against the wall.

"You son of a bitch," James says, "you set me up." Christopher spits in his face.

Sally helps Grimm up off the floor as James punches Christopher in his left ear, dizzying him, and then points a gun right in his face.

I look down and realize James grabbed Grimm's backup when she hit the floor. "James! No. Don't do this. Don't go to jail just for him," I shout.

"It's nice to see you again, James," Christopher goads, "Pull the trigger. Come on, do it. I know you want to." James relaxes his shoulders, takes a deep breath and straightens his gun arm. "Avenge your pathetic wife and her team," Christopher continues, "you should have seen her, all naked and wet, totally surprised to see me. She was in such shock she couldn't even scream."

James's left hand starts tapping against his thigh as if he's debating his next move.

"James, think of Annie and the twins. Don't let them lose you, too," I say as he cocks the hammer of the gun.

"Stay out of this, Ava," James demands.

Both teams are circled around us now, waiting for something to happen. James is still tapping his leg and I take a step toward him. "James, please, put the gun down. Let the cops take care of him," I plead. I take another step.

James doesn't move. I glance at one of the uniforms and tilt my head toward Christopher in a silent *go around the other side and help me* sort of way. He understands.

One more step and I grab James's left arm, startling him, but he puts the gun down. Christopher lunges toward us and there's a loud bang as he falls to the floor, covered in blood.

54

James, May 12th, 2015

ONE OF THE COPS SHOT CHRISTOPHER IN THE LEG. They bandaged him up right away to stem the blood flow, but made sure his pain level was high. Once the ambulance arrived, Ava, Sally and I hopped in Ava's CR-V and followed it to the hospital, Presby of all places.

Christopher never denied any of the murders. In fact, he mocked us for taking almost a week to find him.

"If only poor Allie had had a loving husband like you," he said to me. It took all the willpower I could muster not to smother him with his hospital pillow. "I targeted her first because I figured people wouldn't notice her missing right away. I was right." It's actually kind of smart, in a disgusting sort of way.

Christopher's story was simple: apparently Dr. Bennett had told all the Carters that their father was reacting positively to the chemo, and that beating the cancer was possible. Then, when he suddenly died, Christopher felt like Bennett and his team should be punished for their poor work and for lying to an innocent family.

"Why did you come after me?" I ask him. "I don't work here, I never even met your father. Why try to kill me too?"

"I didn't. I knew you weren't there. I just wanted to scare you," he says with a smile, "and get a few photos of sweet Lacey." And he glances sideways at his pile of clothing.

I instinctively walk over to it, dig through his pockets and find all the missing photos from my hotel room. He cut my face out of every picture. I look up at him, then over to Ava and Sally.

"Been a while since I touched a woman that beautiful. She's been keeping me company this week," he says with a smile.

Ava immediately jumps up and grabs my hand to steer me from the room.

"Don't listen to him. Just don't listen. You're not to talk to him again, understand?" she says to me.

"I understand."

"Good, because I really don't want Grimm to arrest you for murder, no matter how justified it is."

We walk outside into a little courtyard and sit on a park bench. The rain is temporarily replaced with a mist.

After several minutes of silence, Ava says, "So what will you do now?"

"For starters, I'm going to go get my kids and give them the biggest hugs you've ever seen. Then I'm selling our house and moving into some sort of fortress that nobody will ever figure out how to access."

She softly laughs at this, though I'm not really kidding.

* * * * * *

Early the next morning I head over to Ava's place, my car packed and ready to head to Austin. Today she's wearing jeans, a fitted t-shirt and her very old converse sneakers. I realized last night that Ava hasn't been going to work either, that she has devoted all her time to helping me, and I was completely unsure how to thank her.

"I got you something, for letting me stay here. And also for solving Lacey's murder," I say, as I hand her a box and follow her to the couch.

"Actually, *we* solved her murder. You make a great detective, James Abbott," she declares. "If real estate ends up kicking you in the pants, I think we've found your second career!"

"Ha, not likely. I'd rather not be surrounded by murder and death."

"Mmm, right. Me too. You didn't need to get me anything, by the way, I wanted to help."

"It's just something small. Er, Ava, Sally told me about your parents. How they never caught the guy," I say, shaking my head.

"Ah. Yes, well…It was a long time ago. I have made as much peace with it as is possible. But I can't sit here and tell you it doesn't still drive me crazy. Is he out there? Does he know what I look like? Has he seen me? Will he come after me? It's enough to drive anyone crazy. I just couldn't let that happen to you. You have kids to raise."

I think about this for a few seconds, and wonder what story will make it easiest on the kids. The truth? Sure, but maybe without all the gory details.

"Ha! A new pair of converse. I should have guessed that. Thank you," Ava says after opening the present. "You know, this is my third pair. A friend of mine gave me my first pair back when I was a child, he said every good detective needs a comfortable pair of shoes. I bought my second pair in high school, and if you can believe it, these are them. Sixteen years I've worn these shoes. Kind of disgusting, isn't it?"

"That's pretty gross, yeah," I reply.

"Ha. Well thank you, again. This is really unnecessary, but greatly appreciated. Hey when do you get back? I'm having dinner with Clint and a few guys from Briley Commercial next week, want to come?" she asks, with a slight smile.

"Shut up and don't say anything!"

"I won't I won't! But I reserve the right to silently tease you about this for at least one year. A blow job, honestly," she teases, and we both awkwardly laugh.

* * * * * *

One week later, I'm putting my kids to bed at their grandparents' house in Austin, when Ava calls me.

"We have a problem," she begins.

"What is it this time?" I ask.

"James, it's Keith Trammer — Briley Com President — he's dead. Died last night at dinner, right at the table, right in front of us. Poisoned."

THE END